1. This book may be kept three weeks. It is to be
    returned on / before the last date stamped below.
2. A fine of 25c will be charged for every week or
    part of week a book is overdue.

Peter Regan

URBAN HEROES

Illustrated by Terry Myler

THE CHILDREN'S PRESS

All characters are fictional.
Any resemblance to real persons, living or dead,
is purely coincidental.

First published 1992 by
The Children's Press
an imprint of Anvil Books
45 Palmerston Road, Dublin 6

4 6 8 9 7 5

ISBN 0 947962 62 X

Typesetting by Computertype Limited
Printed by Colour Books Limited

*Dedicated to all those
unselfish people who train and manage
schoolboy football teams.
In fact, to everyone who gives up
his or her time to promoting sport
of any kind among our young people.*

1

Shamrock Boys Under-14 soccer team stood waiting for the Bray bus just across the road from Greystones harbour. A cold wind was blowing in off the sea. The choppy white tops of the waves looked icy cold. Usually the team travelled by minibus to away games. But Greystones was only a short distance from Bray, so it was more economical to travel by public transport. Their football bags lay in a pile at the bus-stop. They were fidgety, restless, and most of them kept running across the road to the shop at the front of the Amusement Arcade.

At last the bus came into sight. There was a quick scurry from the shop. A reckless sprint across the road, the icy air steaming from the exertion of their lungs. They grabbed their football bags and rushed in a frenzy to the door of the bus. Their football manager had to calm them down, get them to step on to the bus in a civilized manner. He didn't find it easy.

'Stop pushing.'

'I'm not pushin'.'

'Did you pay the woman in the shop for the sweets?'

'No.'

'Well, you can pay her on the way home. I won't have any of you nicking sweets.'

'I wasn't the only one took sweets, Mr Holmes. Most of the lads took them as well.'

Aware of the futility of it all, Mr Holmes, manager of Shamrock Boys U-14, bit his lip in frustration and ushered the last of the team on to the bus.

The boys stampeded to the top deck and quietened down. They were busy munching chocolate and crisps all the way into Bray. They had a gut feeling the woman wouldn't let them into her shop again. If any Shamrock Boys under-age teams were seen in the vicinity in future she would probably secure her stock of sweets by locking the shop door.

The match about to be played in Bray was an important League fixture. Shamrock Boys needed a win to stay in contention. They were two points adrift of the joint leaders – and a further point behind the team they were due to play in Bray.

Four of the team sat on the seat at the back of the bus. The four – Gavin, Hammer, Luke and Jake – were best friends. Hammer was the tallest, the oldest looking. Gavin was just as well developed, but slightly smaller than Hammer. They looked more like sixteen-year-olds. Luke and Jake were both smaller and looked no more than their true age, fourteen. They didn't mind sitting on the back seat of the bus. It afforded them more scope to talk as a group.

Jake had lost his place on the team at under-10 level. But that didn't stop him going to the matches as a supporter, even to away games, where he would get into conversation and tell a far-fetched story or two, especially if the listener was a stranger. Sometimes when he got fed up, he would go to the back of a ditch and have a smoke. Once his father nearly caught him, but Jake was too smart. He dropped the lighted cigarette into the post-bag his father was carrying and put the mail on fire. It was just as well he was an only child. Another Jake in the family would have been a disaster.

'Are you all right?' Jake asked Luke.

'Course I'm all right.'

'Leave him alone,' whispered Hammer to Jake.

'I was only askin' if he was all right. You saw what he played like last week in the Railway Field, and he's been sulkin' ever since.'

'That's enough,' warned Gavin. 'Leave him alone.'

Normally Jake didn't give out. He had a heart of gold. But he felt for Shamrock Boys. He was a true fan. What he was about to say was cruel, but it was the truth.

'You saw what he did. Started day-dreamin'. Some goalkeeper. Watchin' a train goin' by on the railway embankment during a cup-match. He stood there day-dreamin' and let the ball go into the net.'

'Maybe I did, but at least I can play football and get a game, not like you.'

The statement stung Jake. It knocked the wind out of his sails. But Gavin and Hammer felt he deserved it. He was only getting a taste of his own medicine.

'Never mind slaggin' one another,' cut in Gavin. 'Think of the team. We're hopeless in midfield. Can you think of anyone who might do a good job for us in the middle of the park? I'm fed up gettin' pulled back to do the job. It's about time we got some new players.'

'There's a girl livin' in Applewood Heights. She's a U-14. She's a good footballer,' said Hammer out of the blue.

'A girl!' the other three shouted in disbelief.

'Yes, a girl. And she's good. A class above most boys. I was thinkin' of asking Mr Holmes if he'd let her play for us. She's the right age.'

'But is she really good enough?'

'Course she is. She's new in Greystones. Goes to Loreto in Bray.'

'Mr Holmes couldn't allow it,' said Gavin. 'Remember that case in Bray where the girl wasn't allowed play schoolboy soccer? Well, it was upheld in the Courts, and that's it. Though I heard the FAI had a change of heart. They're lettin' girls up to U-12 level play.'

'Well, that ruling is not fair, especially if the girl is good enough and there's no Schoolgirl League in the area. Rule One:' Hammer sounded as solemn as a judge. 'You can't deprive a child of a game of football. It's a human right.'

'Hammer, you should be a lawyer.'

'I'm going to ask Mr Holmes to let her train with us and play in friendlies.' And the lads knew Hammer wasn't joking. He was determined to see the issue through.

But Gavin had a different suggestion to make. 'Hammer, don't ask Mr Holmes yet. We'll ask her to have a kick-about with us first, and if she's keen enough we'll ask Mr Holmes to let her come trainin'.'

'No strings attached?' asked Hammer.

'No strings attached,' answered Gavin. 'I've nothing against girls playin' football – if they're good enough.'

'Well, this girl is better than good enough.'

'What's her name?'

'Elaine Clarke.'

They had to get off the bus at the bottom of Bray and cross the bridge to the turn-off which led to the People's Park where the match was to be played. The name of the home team was Riverside Boys. It was crucial for Shamrock Boys to win if they wanted to keep their title hopes alive.

The People's Park was set against the backdrop of the Wicklow Mountains and the flow of the Dargle river. There were quaint terraced houses on the roadside.

The pitch itself was pretty awful, hard and stony, and the goal-posts were made of iron. There were no dressing-rooms. Once there had been an old derelict pavilion which backed on to the Dargle. But the roof and walls had been gradually torn down by vandals and sent crashing into the river.

Worse: There was a massive line of trees on the touch-line nearest the road and the ball would sometimes ricochet off the branches and there was no telling where it would come back down. It could even end up behind the player who had kicked it. Also, on the far side of the pitch, there was a low wall on top of the river bank, only yards from the side-line. As likely as not the ball would end up

10

in the river a few times during a match, especially if the home team were hanging on to a narrow lead But apart from its drawbacks the Park was a great place to play in. There was always a crowd, with plenty of atmosphere and incidents to keep the adrenalin going. And when the salmon were surging up the river they attracted the poachers, which occasionally led to the police chasing after them through the Park, their lines and gaffs left in a flurry among the weeds of the river bank.

It took five minutes for Shamrock Boys to walk to the football pitch in the People's Park, Mr Holmes and Hammer taking turns carrying the kit-bag. As well as a stinging March wind there was a touch of drizzle. Some of the team almost hoped the opposition wouldn't show up because, as there were no dressing-rooms, they would have to tog out in the open, beneath the trees.

But the opposition were waiting. They were standing in a slip road behind the bottom goal, hanging around their manager's battered Opel estate car. They intended using the car as a dressing-room. The referee was there as well.

'My God! Just look at who the ref is,' groaned Rasher Murphy, who played right-full. 'It's Harry Hennessy. We won't stand a chance. He'll rob us blind.'

Nobody made a comment. But they all looked in the general direction of the Opel estate, the opposition and the referee. Quite definitely the referee was Harry Hennessy. Even from a distance his vast bulk was apparent. The in joke was that he must have scoured the whole of Ireland for a referee's outfit that fitted. He looked a dead-ringer for Henry the Eighth – with the belly, but without a leg of meat in his grubby hand. Shamrock Boys had several previous run-ins with Harry. To be intellectual; there was history between them.

Mr Holmes, or Lar as some of the boys called him, led the way as far as the half-way line. He went no further. He put the kit-bag down beside one of the trees. 'Let them send the referee's card up to us. I'm not going near that crowd.' There was also history between Lar Holmes and Riverside Boys.

Almost miraculously the drizzle stopped. The boys gathered around Lar to hear the team and to be handed their football gear.

Before Larry had time to make his customary announcement of team selection and general pep-talk, Robert Smyth, the one refined youngster on the Shamrock Boys team, blurted, 'This place is like the Dark Ages.'

'Get your flashlight out then,' interjected a wag.

'To think we train twice a week,' continued Robert, 'to tog out under a tree. It makes me feel like I'm Woody Woodpecker.'

Mr Holmes rhymed off the team. They were to play in a 4-4-2 formation (a four-man defence in front of Luke in goal, four men in midfield, two men up front.) 'Get stuck in early. Don't let them settle on the ball. Keep tight. And we'll take them apart as we please. And don't say nothing to Harry Hennessy. We all know what he is. There's no point in repeating yourselves. It shows a lack of intelligence.'

One of the Riverside substitutes came up from the bottom goal with the referee's card. Larry took it. The other team had already filled it in. He let the players get on with togging out and filled in the card. Just as he finished he looked up. 'And don't forget if you're playing against the wind, play the ball on the ground. And, hey, you,' meaning Jake, 'bring this card back to that effer Hennessy.'

Hammer was told to play in his usual centre-half position and not to play too much football around the edge of his own penalty area, to clear the ball quickly and effectively. Gavin was told to play up front but if things went badly he would be switched to midfield in the sure knowledge he would dictate the flow of the game. Only trouble was, they really hadn't got anybody good enough to take his place up front. But without somebody to control the game from midfield the team wouldn't function properly; it would lose its shape and, more importantly, possession of the ball.

Jake, who was giving a hand by putting the players' clothes into their bags and sheltering the lot beneath the tree in case it would start raining again, looked down the pitch, to where the Opel estate was parked. Some of the Riverside boys were already out on the pitch. They were having a kick-about.

'Look,' he shouted. 'They've got Chopper Doyle playin'. I thought he was suspended.'

'He *is* suspended. The pup! There hasn't been a ball kicked and already there's trouble.' Mr Holmes was livid. He felt like going down the pitch and giving the other team manager a rollicking.

'What are you goin' to do about it?' asked Jake.

'Do? I'll do nothing. But if we lose there's goin' to be a protest.'

'Don't protest. We'll beat them on the pitch,' said Gavin.

'Yeah. We'll beat them fair and square,' added Hammer.

'We'll marmalize them,' throbbed Rasher Murphy. 'That Chopper Doyle is a pure half-savage. Just look at him.'

The gallery of Shamrock players looked.

All the Riverside boys were out on the pitch by now. All except Chopper Doyle were involved in the kick-about. He didn't seem to be interested in the ball. He was checking his football laces to make sure they were good and tight so as to make a strong impact on the game.

Shamrock Boys trotted out in their all-green strip and had their own kick-about while they waited for the game to start.

The referee came on to the pitch. He looked awesome, like an all-in wrestler about to have a seizure.

'That man'd do anything for drink,' shouted Jake.

Harry Hennessy glared at Jake before turning and

13

calling the two captains together for the toss.

Hammer lost the toss.

Riverside Boys elected to play with the wind. They changed ends and lined up for the centre.

Mr Holmes had a rethink. 'Gavin, switch to midfield and tell Robert Smyth to play up front.'

Then he made a calculated misjudgement; he gave Jake the linesman's flag sent over from the centre circle by Harry Hennessy.

'What's this for?'

'Do the line.'

'Why don't you do it?'

'I want nothing to do with that Harry Hennessy.'

'He'll overrule me.'

'Let him. It might put a strain on his heart.'

Robert Smyth lined up with his fellow front-man to centre the ball.

The referee synchronized his watch, blew his whistle and the game was on.

The wind dictated the pattern of the game. It suited Shamrock Boys more than Riverside. Although they had the best two players in the League in Gavin and Hammer, all round Riverside were a better balanced team, with a lot of good players in their ranks. In contrast some of the Shamrock players were plodders.

Basically Shamrock Boys were a 'spoilers' team. They had a low skill level and used spoiling tactics to contain the opposition. There was very little shape to their game; it was more of a kick and rush effort. The only touches of class came from Gavin and Hammer and the team depended on them to win matches.

Being a spoiling team, the wind didn't put them out that much, except that they had to play against it in the first half. Riverside Boys found the conditions much harder. With the wind at their backs they were overhitting the ball. A lot of balls went harmlessly wide over the end-line.

Jake wasn't having much luck on the line. Every time he put the flag up for off-side Harry Hennessy ignored him. There were two blatant off-sides. On the second, Jake shouted, 'Ref, you're not fit to referee a dog-fight!'

'What did you say?'

'You're not fit to ref a dog-fight.'

'Hand that flag over to someone else.'

Jake handed the linesman's flag to a reluctant Mr Holmes.

The game restarted. The ball went into the river. The Riverside Boys manager went after it. Someone threw a replacement ball on to the pitch. While the manager was gone Riverside scored from a wind-assisted shot that clattered in off the underside of the cross-bar.

Robert Smyth recentred the ball. It was played back to Gavin. He held it, played it short to his left, ran into space for a return pass. But his team-mate wasn't able to play the ball through. Riverside regained possession. Gavin ran back and took up a covering position, just in front of the back four. Riverside knocked the ball in across the edge of the penalty area. A defender made a half clearance. The ball fell to Gavin. He held it. Tried to wait for his own players to get forward. He carried the ball out of defence, beating three players, and played a through ball behind the opposition's back four. But Robert Smyth was too slow to read the situation. Riverside Boys took up possession again.

It was getting close to half-time. Luke, in goal, wasn't too full of confidence. He was beginning to fumble the ball. He let one easy shot slip through his hands. Hammer cleared it off the line.

'Hold that ball,' screeched Mr Holmes at poor Luke.

It was obvious Luke's heart wasn't in the game. What little bit of confidence he had was well and truly shattered. Hammer tried to talk him through the crisis:

'What's wrong?'

'He's always shoutin', and it's usually at me. I don't have to take this stick. I got enough of it from him last Saturday in the Railway Field. I don't want more.'

Luke was still brooding over what had happened the week before in the home Cup game at the Railway Field. His concentration had lapsed and he was to blame for a soft goal going in. The play had been in the other half of the Field. A train went by on the railway embankment. Luke became mesmerized by the train. The play switched from the other half and a goal went in against him. He didn't even realize the ball was in the net. He stood transfixed, looking up at the high embankment as the Dublin-Rosslare train trundled by. One of his team-mates had to take the ball out of the net, tap him on the shoulder and bring him to his senses. Mr Holmes was furious. Only for Gavin they would have lost the match. He scored two goals in the last few minutes and Shamrock Boys won 2-1. Luke was soured. He didn't want to play any more. But he kept his thoughts to himself.

Just before half-time Riverside scored a second goal. For Shamrock Boys, two goals down and with the wind behind them in the second half, it could have been worse.

Mr Holmes really bullied the players during the half-time break. He had no finesse. He wasn't a good manager.

Jake didn't stand around to hear the half-time pep-talk. He went up to the top of the Park, to a patch of concrete ground, where there was a toss-school in progress. Jake had a few coins and the men let him join in. He won a few bob and went back to the match. It was good to win, but he knew better than to get involved in gambling again. It was a habit he could do without. Jake, being Jake, was willing to try anything once. There would be no repeat performance, not ever. Toss-schools were bad news; even Jake could see that.

By the time he got back to the pitch the second half was a third of the way through. Gavin had moved from midfield into a striker's role. He was probing hard, and getting in with some blistering shots. Hammer was pushing from the centre-half position into the midfield as much as he could. Robert Smyth was combining well with Gavin. It was a much improved performance from Shamrock Boys in the second half. Thankfully Luke wasn't getting that much to do in goal. And the flack from Mr Holmes had stopped.

But Shamrock Boys were still losing 2-nil. Even with Gavin's brilliance the ball just would not go in.

So far, Chopper Doyle hadn't made much of an impression on the game. But that was to change.

Bugsy Ryan, the lightweight Shamrock Boys wide midfield player, was going through with the ball. Chopper clattered him with an over-the-ball tackle. Surprisingly the referee took heed. He booked Chopper.

Two minutes later Chopper did something similar. He pole-axed Gavin. Harry Hennessy sent him off.

Chopper wasn't too put out. He strolled back to the make-shift dressing-room; the Opel estate. On the way he picked up a lollipop stick off the ground. The side door of the Opel was open. He got in, took his boots off and climbed in behind the steering wheel. He had a look to see if anyone was watching. Next thing, he put the lollipop stick into the ignition and turned it. The engine spurted to life. He put the car into gear, released the handbrake and drove off.

Robert Smyth had put the ball in the back of the net. Harry blew for an infringement on the goalkeeper.

'Goal, ref!' slated Gavin.

'No goal! Your number 7 infringed the goalkeeper. Are you disputin' the decision?'

No answer.

The goal was disallowed.

Liam Glynn, the Riverside manager, breathed a sigh of relief. He was very pleased with the referee's decision. He was usually pleased with Harry Hennessy's decisions.

'Liam,' a mousey eleven-year-old was tugging at Liam Glynn's sleeve. 'Chopper Doyle's goin' off in your car.'

'He's what?'

'He's goin' for a drive in your car.'

The Riverside manager swung around. The Opel estate drove by on the road outside the Park railings. Chopper Doyle's smiling face showed in the car window.

He blew the car-horn as he passed the centre-circle.

The Riverside manager almost collapsed with shock. He checked his pockets to make sure the car keys weren't missing. Then he remembered, he remembered Chopper messing one night in the car during training. He had started it with a lollipop stick. The barrel was worn and almost anything that fitted would turn the ignition.

As he watched the car drive towards Main Street the Riverside manager's only consolation was at least Chopper was driving in a straight line and seemed to have control over the vehicle.

The players on the pitch, as yet, knew nothing about Chopper's escapade. The game continued uninterrupted, though Liam Glynn had lost all interest. He was too fretful for his Opel. Shamrock Boys were destined not to score; their League hopes seemed about to take a real tumble. As a last resort, they could protest on the grounds that Riverside Boys had played a suspended player, and Mr Holmes vowed to do so. But as would be learned, when the protest was heard, the Riverside manager had pulled a fast one: Chopper Doyle's name was not on the referee's card; he had played in a different name. The protest was thrown out.

Just as the game ended, Chopper Doyle arrived back at the pitch. He was in the back of a squad-car. The Opel followed behind. A Garda was driving it. Chopper had been spotted by the Gardai going up the steep gradient of the Putland Hill from the sea front. They had flagged him down and brought him back, back to the People's Park where he was the centre of attention.

Chopper Doyle had suddenly become a cult figure.

For Luke, the final drift away from football came just after the match in the People's Park ended. Three youngsters came into the Park. One clutched a cardboard box.

'What's in the box?' asked Luke.

"A grizzle and a white.'

'What's that?'

'They're pigeons.'

'Give's a look.'

The child partly opened the box and held his hand over the gap. Luke squinted in. He could see the curved shape of the pigeons' heads. He was impressed. 'Where did you get them?'

'Down in the harbour. We looped them. They're youngsters, put out on a trainin' flight. The strays always come down around the harbour. There's loads of grit there for the pigeons to pick at.'

The three could see Luke was interested. They took out a loop and showed him how to use it.

'It's fishin' line really. Don't get cat-gut 'cause it cuts into the pigeons. Get the cord stuff that's on a handline. Loop it on the end an' put it on the ground with some pigeon corn in the loop. When the pigeon walks in an' picks at the corn pull on the line an' the loop'll tighten around its leg.'

Already Luke's mind was working. Pigeons were something different, and they could be raced. They would be a good substitute for football. He wouldn't be bawled out like last Saturday. He could make mistakes, do what he liked, and there would be nobody there to 'give out' if things went wrong. The whole idea appealed to him.

'. . . If you catch strays you've to keep them locked up for a few weeks, 'cause if you don't they'll only go back to where they belong . . .'

Luke listened with interest. Then the three kids were gone. They shouted back that they might see him in the harbour during the summer. They said that Saturday nights, after the pigeon races, were the best time to catch them. Luke went back over to where the rest of the team were getting changed but he said nothing about giving up playing football, not yet.

Just as he got back to the lads, a poorly dressed man began to rummage on the ground near where the players were dressing. He had been watching the match. He got talking to Gavin and Hammer.

'You're two good prospects . . . plenty of ability. You mightn't think much of me. But listen, I give sound advice. The two of you are good 'uns. Don't get big-headed though. Look after yourselves and respect the game. Make use of your skill and don't abuse it. Ever hear of Jim Baxter?'

'No, never. Who is he?'

'He was the greatest wing-half that ever lived. Jim Baxter was Scottish and played all his football north of the Border until he went to England to play for Nottingham Forest. That finished Jim Baxter.'

'What do you mean?'

'He wasn't able to handle the high life. He went to bits. And he ain't the only one. There're hundreds out there like him. Some got fame before they blew it. Others never even get that far. What I'm tryin' to say is, put the effort in and don't abuse the system. Like I said, you're two good 'uns. Probably good enough to play schoolboy for Ireland and maybe good enough to go into the pro game in England someday. Well, I'll be seein' yous. And take heed of what I say. I mightn't look much, but I give good advice. You see, I know what it's all about – the good and the bad. Understand?'

'Kind of.'

The man went on a little bit more before moving off to a

fresh location over near the wall at the river to continue his rummaging. He began to repeat himself. He told the two lads they had what it would take, that they could go all the way, even play for Ireland. The pitfall would be that they would have to look after themselves, neither drink nor smoke, nor keep the wrong kind of company; train hard and be dedicated.

Gavin and Luke were chuffed at what the man had said. It was nice to have someone say that kind of thing to them. It gave them a boost. Little did they realize that the raggedly dressed man had once been a professional footballer who had withdrawn into himself and had become reclusive.

Jake, who had been listening with impatience, told them to hurry up as he wanted to go up the town to buy a few guitar strings for a second-hand guitar someone had given him. This was one of the first intimations the lads had that Jake was seriously interested in music. He wanted to buy a plectrum as well. The money he won in the toss-school would more than cover the outlay.

The four lads excused themselves and left the team just beyond the bridge at the bottom of Main Street. They walked up the town, looked into shop windows and went into a chipper while Jake bought his guitar-strings and plectrum elsewhere.

As they progressed Luke kept an eye open for a shop where he could buy some pigeon food if need be. He said nothing to the others about his intentions. He was totally fed up with football, especially the way Lar Holmes always seemed to be picking on him and on nobody else. He wouldn't show up for training. Neither would he bother going to any matches. The penny would drop; they'd know he wasn't interested in playing football any more, and they wouldn't come looking for him. He'd have to see about getting a few pigeons. He'd have to ask for some advice on how to look after them. As of now football was a thing of the past for Luke and nothing was going to make him change his mind.

When Gavin and Hammer got home they discovered that word had been left for them that they were to play for one of Shamrock Boys older teams the following day. They were glad. They had nothing much to do on a Sunday.

Jake stayed at home and practised on his somewhat shoddy second-hand guitar.

Luke dreamed of becoming a top pigeon racer.

But Hammer had one other thing on his mind. He wanted to get in touch with Elaine Clarke, to tell her of a 'mess match' he'd arranged for Tuesday after school. The match would be played on the green in the estate where he lived. Most of the lads who lived around would be playing. And he wanted Gavin there. Gavin would have to be there. He wanted Gavin to see how good Elaine Clarke was.

2

On Tuesday Hammer was waiting on the green at 4.30. All the usual lads who played football were there. The pitch was compact, with a set of portable goal-posts provided by the local tenants' association. The match was to be a seven-a-side affair, with most of the players in the fourteen to sixteen age bracket.

Gavin was there too, purely as a spectator.

The game began at 4.45. Hammer held back the start until Elaine Clarke got to the green. That way the sides would balance out. She had phoned Hammer the previous night to say that she wouldn't be able to make it until five as she would have to come on after school. While he waited Hammer spent the time talking to Gavin.

'There's talk Lar Holmes might get kicked out as manager of the team,' said Gavin.

'Who told you that?'

'It's rumoured. Wind got back to the committee. They've heard Luke has left. They're afraid more will go.'

'Who'd be manager then?'

'Don't know. Probably another crank like Lar.'

Before they had time to speculate any further Elaine Clarke came into view. She was wearing a track-suit, very fashionable, very eye-catching, and an expensive pair of Puma training shoes. A sports-bag was slung from her shoulders. Her hair was auburn, with a tidy fringe at the front. She looked too feminine to be a footballer.

She walked up to where the boys were standing. Gavin could see that Hammer was attracted to her.

'Sorry I'm late,' she said. She spoke with an English accent.

'You're not late. You're dead on time.'

Hammer introduced Gavin. 'My friend, Gavin Byrne.'

'Shane told me all about you,' smiled Elaine.

'He did?'

As a point of interest, Hammer's name was Shane Teale.

'You're English,' said Gavin.

'Does that worry you?'

'No, just surprised.'

'I was born in Wexford. We came back to Ireland two months ago.'

'What part of England did you live in?'

'Coventry . . . It's a bit chilly. You don't mind if I play in my track-suit, do you?'

Gavin laughed.

Elaine knew what Gavin was thinking. Probably thought that she couldn't play at all. That she was just a pretty girl with an eye for sports fashion. Well, he could have a rethink. She decided on a change of strategy. She put the sports-bag on the ground and unzipped it. Inside Gavin could see a towel and some surplus gear. Oh, and there was a copy of *Smash Hits*. 'On second thoughts I don't think I'll wear my track-suit. It's not that cold.' She unzipped the top of the track-suit. Took it off, and then the bottom. Underneath she wore a black and amber football kit. There was a number 7 on the back.

'You've played a bit of club football?' queried Gavin.

'Not here. In England. It's not my only sport, though. I'm also into athletics.'

Gavin was beginning to sense that Elaine wasn't an average type of girl. He couldn't wait for her to get out on the pitch to see what she could do with a football.

Within seconds he had his answer. She was explosive. Down right brilliant. No wonder she wore number 7 on her jersey. She had the exact same style as Kenny Dalglish. She could hold the ball up like him. Twist and turn in the penalty area just like him. And above all, score quality

24

goals just like him. Admittedly the opposition wasn't world class. But she was up against three of Shamrock Boys U-16 team, plus two from the U-15 team. She more than held her own; she made a show of them. Her best score came with her back to goal. She took control of the ball, pivoted, and sent a cracking shot into the top right-hand corner of the net.

Hammer was delighted. He could see Gavin was impressed. Gavin was: He had never seen a girl soccer player as good as her. Neither had any of the others.

When the game was over most of the boys were too embarrassed to say anything. But not Gavin. He shook her hand. As for Hammer he felt so proud. After all it was he who had discovered her. He'd been out on his own one day kicking a ball about. She had come over and started talking to him. Next thing, she had joined in. He had thought about her a lot since. Now he was trying to build up the courage to ask her out on a date.

'You said you were into athletics,' said Gavin. 'Which are you better at, runnin' or football?'

'It's just much of a muchness.' She finished towelling herself and put her track-suit back on. 'I used to play a lot of soccer in England. But there are no teams for girls over here. So I hope to concentrate on athletics instead.'

'There are girls' teams in Dublin. Join one of those.'

'I'm not sure I really want to. People over here don't seem to take girl soccer players seriously. I don't like that. Anyway I'll be fifteen in September and I think I'll concentrate on athletics. Girls are more appreciated on the running track than on a football pitch. My father is getting me into an athletic club in Dublin soon.'

'What's the name of the club?'

'Crusaders.'

'Well, if you like,' suggested Gavin, 'you can come down and train in our soccer club until you have everything sorted out.'

'I don't think I would like that. All boys and no girls. It wouldn't be my scene.'

'Maybe you're right. Most of the lads are only messers anyway. And as for Lar Holmes, he'd drive you around the twist with his moanin'.'

'Who's Lar Holmes?'

'Sad to say, he's our manager. Ex-manager hopefully.'

Just then Hammer asked Elaine for a date.

Gavin could hardly believe his ears. You'd at least think he'd wait until there was no one around.

'I'll think about it,' replied Elaine. She picked up the sports-bag. 'I'll give it serious consideration,' she laughed. 'See you around.' With that she was gone. They watched her turn between a row of houses and vanish out of sight. She looked a pretty picture.

'So that's why you asked her down here – for a date.'

'No, it was for football. You told me to.'

'You're not foolin' me.'

'No, football. Honest . . . Hey, you're jealous!'

The two lads looked hard at one another. Turned on their heels, and, like Elaine, went home.

Gavin and Hammer always trained very hard. Often they trained on their own; on the gravelly South Beach and, even more severe, across the punishing mountain terrain of Bray Head. Sometimes Luke and Jake would go with them, but only part of the way. Luke would soon get bored and sit on a rock and look out to sea. Jake would keep him company, have a smoke and toss a few ideas around in his head for a song he was thinking of composing. They would wait and catch Gavin and Hammer on the way back.

They had two runs on Bray Head. The straight run was along the Cliff Walk between Bray and Greystones, and back again. The second, more difficult run, which they mostly used during the summer, before the season began, went out along the Cliff Walk until it came to a track which zigzagged through the heather right up to the top of Bray Head. It followed a wide path on top all the way to the Cross, where there were two ways down; straight down through the rocks, or around the crest of the Head into a wood that was like a stud on a belt around the waist of the mountain. Eventually, they would come down to a path through the wood. In the seaward direction, it led out almost directly beside where the Cliff Walk began. From there they would complete the circle by running back to Greystones along the Cliff Walk.

Gavin and Hammer knew that all the sweat, agony and toil of jogging on South Beach and running over Bray Head was not the complete answer to football training. It was only good only in so far as it promoted general fitness. Exercises, sprints and circuit training were more beneficial. And of course, plenty of practice with a football was essential, whether touch football in small groups or ball discipline alone.

Gavin and Hammer were natural footballers who had unknowingly honed their skills at a younger age while playing street football, sometimes using a lampost as a goal, or, on their own, spending long hours kicking a ball against a wall.

Two weeks after the match on the green Hammer made a second effort to date Elaine Clarke. But Gavin spoiled everything. Unknown to Hammer Gavin had already asked her out. The situation was awkward, so, rather than disappoint one, she declined both their offers. But she began to train with them on their runs over Bray Head, which she preferred to training with Shamrock Boys at the Railway Field. The runs over the Head suited her fine. Anyway, Shamrock Boys trained at night and she had too much homework to do. Also, there was the matter of running with Crusaders.

So far Elaine had not met Jake or Luke. But on hearing

that Jake played the guitar, she asked a few questions about him. This show of interest made Gavin and Hammer feel jealous and the close friendship between the boys was put on hold as questions were fielded.

'You wouldn't like Jake.'

'He's a messer.'

'He's a bit of a spacer.'

'How come?'

'He's always doin' whacky things.'

'Like what?'

'Like what's spaced-out – mad.'

'And what about Luke?'

'He only thinks of his pigeons.'

'He's a bore.'

'Yeah, a bore, especially far as girls would be concerned. You'd find him a real bore. Take it from us, you just wouldn't be interested in meetin' Luke.'

'I don't know . . . Jake seems to be a real character.'

Hammer had enough of talking about Jake and Luke. He decided to change the subject: 'We're having a friendly match on Saturday, at home. Why don't you come down?'

'I've already told you. I'd prefer to play on a girls' team. It's a bit embarrassing when you're the only girl. Anyway, would your manager allow it?'

'He doesn't mind. Said to come. Anyway, it's only a friendly. You're entitled to play.'

'Right, I'll be there.'

Elaine left them at the gate to her house. She could see her mother just inside the front window. She waved to her and went in.

3

Elaine was at the Railway Field in plenty of time for the friendly match. She was well received. Even Mr Holmes was polite to her. The opposition, who were from Ballybrack, didn't pay much heed, not until they realized she was about to play. Immediately they took a more active interest, regarding her as something of a curiosity. But Elaine wasn't too put out. She half expected a few stares and whispers. She looked around her, glancing at the steep railway embankment from which the field took its name. There was a certain romanticism about the railway line on top of the embankment. She noted the faded white paint of the goal-posts, the worn grass carpeting the flanks, the chafed centre of the pitch where thin patches of grass showed above the black surface clay, and grimaced at the muddy goal areas. Then Hammer came over to her and took her to the dressing-rooms, just inside the entrance to the field.

'I like it,' said Elaine.

'What?'

'The pitch, of course. It's a bit muddy. But everywhere is at this time of year.'

'You're to tog out in here.'

Hammer had taken her into a small room, one used by match officials such as the referee or linesmen.

'Grand.'

'You don't mind?'

'No. It's not really like being part of a team, but you're not to blame. No one's to blame.'

'The lads are all glad you're here. They've all heard how good you are. They want you on the team.'

'What about the manager?'

'He wants you too. But he's under pressure.'

'What do you mean?'

'Some of the players don't like him. He can be hard on players – shoutin' and that. The club committee is thinkin' of gettin' rid of him. Anyway, it's got nothing to do with you. Enjoy the match.'

Elaine had taken her boots from the sports-bag. She held them in her hand and inspected the studs. 'Is this the only club you've played for?'

'Yes, we all started out here. This is it: Shamrock Boys, the Railway Field, Greystones.'

'Ever think of playing for another club?'

'No. But Gavin has.'

'You're loyal then?'

'Listen, I started out with this club when I was eight. It's the only club I've ever known.'

Elaine didn't answer immediately. She was thinking about changing studs, putting in longer ones, ones that would give more grip. 'Don't get so upset! You're a good player. Other clubs go chasing after good players. Have you ever been asked to leave Shamrock Boys?'

'Yes, a few times.'

'Has Gavin?'

'Yes.'

'There comes a time when a good player should move on.'

'What d'you mean?'

'I'm talking about ambition and wanting to get on. You'd like to get on, wouldn't you?'

'You mean in a football sense?'

'Yes. I know what it's all about. But being a girl, people make it hard for me. You're a boy. Get out there and go for it by joining a bigger club. One that has influence. Shamrock Boys may be a nice club but they're not going anywhere, except up a back alley. It may not be their fault but that's the politics of football. Believe me, I know.'

Hammer's head was in a spin. The girl was smart. Maybe too damn smart. She was talking way over his head. 'See you outside,' he said and left the room.

What Elaine said was on Hammer's mind all the time as he stripped. Leave the team? He, Gavin, Luke and Jake had joined Shamrock Boys together. He remembered the first practice match only too well. It was just like flicking a switch and it all came back.

When they were eight, Gavin's father had brought them to the Railway Field, just across the road from Greystones harbour, for a try-out for Shamrock Boys U-9 team. Jake was already in his football gear. He had togged out at home. The others had their football bags slung from their shoulders – the bags were almost as big as themselves. Gavin's father couldn't help smiling. But the four lads took it all very seriously. They huffed and chattered, and couldn't wait to get to the pitch.

When they got to the Railway Field there were twenty young hopefuls already there. They were brought into the dressing-rooms to tog out. Luke stood embarrassed in a corner. He whispered to Hammer. He could not tie his football laces. Hammer duly performed the necessary, and they joined the noisy throng as all twenty-four ran out on to the pitch. The two men in charge found it hard to keep the kids still as they picked two teams. And when the game started the youngsters chased like sheep after the ball. Afterwards, the men had trouble getting the jerseys back. They all wanted to keep them.

'Are we good enough, Mister?'

'Yeah.'

'When do we come back?'

'Next Saturday, same time.'

'Same place?'

'Yeah, same place. See you, then.'

The kids scampered off to the main road.

'That was great, wasn't it?'

'Deadly. We were Liverpool and you were Everton.'

'Know what?'

'What?'

'Can't wait to play in a league. They'll have real refs, not like that man in his clothes. And know what?'

'What?'

'The man didn't even know the rules.'

'How?'

'I scored a goal. I handled it and he gave it. Can't wait until next Saturday. Can you?'

Neither could Gavin, Hammer, Luke and Jake.

This had been their introduction to organized football. Six years later, they were all, with the exception of Luke, as football mad as ever.

Now Elaine Clarke was suggesting to Hammer that he should turn his back on Shamrock Boys. That his and Gavin's talent had outgrown the club and that it was time to move on. But how could he turn his back on his own team? He knew Gavin might; Gavin was very ambitious. And Mr Holmes's insensitive remarks and bouts of temper weren't exactly encouraging players to stay.

Hammer felt he owed Shamrock Boys something.

If there had been no Shamrock Boys, he would never have played soccer. Nor would Gavin. The club had given them the opportunity. It was all right for Elaine Clarke, a stranger, to talk. She had her roots elsewhere. His roots were with Shamrock Boys.

When Elaine came out of the dressing-room Ballybrack were already on the pitch. They were in a huddle around their manager. Although only a friendly they were taking the game seriously. They were top of their section in the Dublin Schoolboys' League. As all the Corporation and County Council pitches in Dublin had been closed for the previous two weeks, they were badly in need of a match Their manager, a train-driver on the DART line, had arranged the game at the last minute. The previous Wednesday he had pulled into Salthill station and noticed Lar Holmes standing on the opposite platform. He got out of the cab and ran across the pedestrian bridge. The match was quickly arranged. He sprinted back over the bridge, got back into the cab, released the driver's brake and drove the train on down the line towards Howth. He had seen Shamrock Boys play before. The team had stuck in his mind – not so much the team, but the playing abilities of Gavin and Hammer. He reckoned he'd give the Dublin Schoolboys' League a fair old dust-up with those two lads in his team. Pity he couldn't have them. But, at least, he knew they existed.

As for the game:

Gavin had just played a thirty-yard pass with pin-point precision. Three minutes later he scored a solo goal. He beat the defence and planted the ball in the corner of the net with a wicked right-foot drive.

'Play the ball through, Gavin.' This time it was Elaine.

'Play the ball through,' she repeated.

Gavin played the ball into the hole behind the defence. Elaine ran on to it. Brought it to the edge of the area. She hesitated. The goalkeeper advanced. She calmly chipped the ball over his head, into the net. Goal number two.

Shamrock Boys were playing well, better than any time lately. Lar Holmes watched from the touch-line. He wasn't growling. He was smiling.

Further down the side-line, two of Shamrock Boys committee members stood passively. They weren't on talking terms with Lar.

Ballybrack pulled a goal back.

Then another. And another.

2-3. Eight minutes to go.

The two committee members began to square up to Lar. They told him a new manager would be taking over his team as of the next game. They put it down to Lar's tantrums and their fear the team would break up.

'That so?' defied Lar.

'Yes. That's so.'

'Well, know what you can do?'

'We know. And you can do the same, Lar.'

'My pleasure.'

The pitch had become very sticky. Elaine was prompting Shamrock Boys to make a last-ditch fightback. She had the makings of a great captain. And she could lead by example. She told Rasher Murphy to stop camping on the half-way line, get forward on the overlap when the pressure was off the back, and act as a supporting wing-player.

'Come on. You're quick enough. You can cross a ball. Get the lead out and get forward. Your mother didn't rear you to sit on your backside.'

Rasher went as red as a beetroot. But he woke up and did things nobody thought he was capable of, not even himself. He played like a terrier down the right-hand flank. 'Open the gates, I'm comin', I'm comin',' And he sent over a centre that skimmed the Ballybrack cross-bar.

Then with two minutes to go Robert Smyth scored from a pass by Elaine. He turned around and chased up the field after her. He hugged her.

'Jumpin' lizards!' said Rasher. 'I wouldn't mind playin' football with her every week. And the more goals we'd score the better. Just think of it.'

'Cut it out, Rasher.'

A minute and a half later the full-time whistle went. The Ballybrack team changed, got into their minibus and went back to South County Dublin.

The Shamrock Boys players hung around outside the dressing-rooms. Word had gone out that Mr Holmes was no longer manager of the team.

By this time Jake had arrived. He had been at home practising on his guitar, and got so completely wrapped up in what he was doing that the time flew. It was over two hours before he came to and remembered the match. Immediately he rushed to the Railway Field.

'What's goin' to happen to Lar Holmes?'

'Who cares?'

'I wonder who the new manager will be?'

'Hope he's not like that Paul Malone we had when we were under tens.'

'Spare the thought. He reminded me of St Patrick, the way he had us in his garden in the evenin' sayin' the Angelus and a decade of the Rosary. Thank God, he went to live in Cork.'

'Jake said different. Jake said he left to become a missionary in Africa and to train the Cameroons.'

'Who'd believe that?'

'Anyone who knelt in a garden at six o'clock and had to say the Angelus.'

Just then Elaine came out of the pavilion. Gavin introduced her to Jake.

Then Mr Holmes came out. He hadn't got the kit-bag. He was empty-handed.

'I suppose you've heard you're getting a new manager?'

'We've heard,' said Gavin coldly.

'Well, all I can say is I did my best. Maybe you weren't happy with me. I put the time in. You lot wouldn't appreciate what it takes to run a team – the effort that has to be put in. Standing there getting soaked in the rain – training and marking pitches, running around getting you lot out on the pitch, digging into my pocket to pay referees' fees and sometimes paying the difference on minibus fares. No, thanks. Football manager! I was only a glorified baby-sitter! What have you got to say about that?'

No one answered him. They hadn't got anything to say.

Mr Holmes was gone. Or was he? He was talking to Elaine. 'Joining a girls' team?' he asked her.

'There are none around here.'

'How come you know so much about soccer?'

'My father coached Coventry City.'

'Think it's unfair not letting girls play on boys' teams?'

'It's unfair if girls have the ability. I know there are other problems but everything should be based on ability.'

'Well, I'd play you. I'd keep you on the team until I was told to stop. Then I'd ring the newspapers. You heard about the girl in Bray who was stopped from playing?'

'Yes, I heard.'

'Well, the whole thing would blow up again, only this time much stronger. There can be differences between boys' and girls' footballing capabilities. But when the differences are clouded by discrimination, that's wrong. You've got the talent to become a top-class player. You could set the ball rolling for equality in the soccer world. You could be a real hot potato.'

'Be a guinea pig? I don't want that.'

'Pity. You could be used as a test case. If things don't work out, why don't you give a hand with training some of Shamrock Boys younger teams?'

'I was to join an athletic club in Dublin, but I can't until summer. But I don't really have the time.'

'Make the time. It would help to keep you involved.'

Lar Holmes turned to leave.

'Mr Holmes, the players said you were too cranky.'

'Maybe I was.'

'Mr Holmes, I think you've been misunderstood.'

'I'd go along with that. They use you and misuse you. And then it's good-bye.'

Lar Holmes took one last look at the Railway Field. He shrugged his shoulders. In a way he felt relief. Relief that all the running around was finished with. That all the chasing after players and the aggro of protests and ill-feeling cause by running a schoolboy team were over.

As surely as he left the Railway Field there was no coming back. He was gone from the game he loved so much. And in the end it didn't matter in the least. At the death there was nothing. It surprised him how easy it was to walk away.

After Mr Holmes left, Gavin, Hammer and Jake walked up the road with Elaine, past the fire-station and the old picture-house. Elaine lived over towards Redford in one of the more upper-class housing estates. She was a lot posher than most of the girls they knew. Maybe it was her English accent. It was becoming clearer by the day that soccer was the common denominator responsible for drawing them together. Only for soccer they would have moved in completely different worlds.

All went quietly enough (a lot of small talk) until they got near the fork in the road at Redford. Then Gavin mentioned the conversation Elaine had had with Hammer in the dressing-rooms, about leaving Shamrock Boys.

'Elaine, we know our own minds. Don't interfere. We've got our ambitions. We're not brainless. We'll know when it's time to leave and how to go about it.'

'I was only trying to help. If you feel bad about it . . .'

'We don't feel bad. I'm only tryin' to put you right. Your kind of talk wouldn't be appreciated around the club. Just don't talk about things like that.'

'Is that why Lar Holmes got the bullet? Because he was honest?'

'Elaine, that's a different kettle of fish.'

'No, it's not so different.'

'You're being pig-headed.'

'I'm not!'

'Elaine, we've been around this club all our lives. You're only here a few hours. Anyway, let's forget about it.'

'Well, have it your way. But I'll bet any money that you won't be with Shamrock Boys in two years' time. Hammer will. You won't.'

Gavin said nothing. The tension was tangible.

'Why don't we go for a run over Bray Head tomorrow?'

suggested Hammer. He was trying to defuse matters. Get off the subject as quickly as possible.

'I wouldn't mind goin' too,' interjected Jake.

Gavin expressed surprise. Usually Jake detested all forms of exercise except football. 'Jake, you haven't gone for a run over Bray Head for at least three years.'

'But I'll go tomorrow.' He wanted to see more of this new girl, Elaine. But so far she hadn't said whether she would go on the run or not. 'I'm thinkin' of goin' into trainin' again.' What if she wouldn't go? Well, if she wouldn't, as sure as hell he'd stay in bed.

'Elaine?' It was Hammer again. 'Are you comin' ?'

'Yes, I'll go.'

'Good. Pick you up outside your house at eleven.'

Jake could hardly wait. First thing he'd do when he got home he'd look for his runners. He hadn't worn them for almost a year. He didn't even think of the horrendous strain of the run over Bray Head. All he could think of was Elaine. The last time he had been on top of Bray Head he had been on his own. He had walked along a gully covered by ferns when all of a sudden he was confronted by a wild billy-goat with horns the size of an armchair. He clambered out with the goat in hot pursuit. Only for a tree within grabbing distance he would have been finished. He scrambled up the tree and hung on for dear life. The goat stomped and rubbed its horns off the trunk for what seemed like hours. But in the end it went away. Other goats came on the scene and the billy-goat tagged along after them. It was just as well, because as a last resort Jake had threatened to pee down from the top of the tree.

Eleven-o'clock Sunday they went for the run. The effort almost killed Jake. The pace was really fast. But, at least, there were no goats in the vicinity of Bray Head.

Half way through the run he got winded and flung himself to the ground.

'Did I ever tell you about the time when Jake was nine

years old?' said Hammer.

'No,' said Elaine, amused, conscious of Jake's mute appeal for a rest stop.

'He went to confession to an old priest who was very stern, very strict. There he was in the darkness tremblin' like a leaf. Then the grill opened . . .'

' "What is it, child? Speak!"

' "I've come to tell you about me grandpa."

' "Have you no sins to confess?"

' "No, I just want to tell you about me grandpa."

' "Has he done something wrong?"

' "No . . . me grandfather was the strongest man in Greystones."

' "Quite so. Quite so."

' "Once he was drivin' a horse and cart back to the farmyard where he worked. When he got back the gate was locked, so he undid the horse from the cart and lifted the cart over the wall."

' "How high was the wall?" '

' "Fifteen foot."

' "Hmmmm . . ."

' "Then know what he did?"

' "No, what?"

' "He lifted the horse over the wall."

' "Child, for your lie . . ."

' "It's not a lie, Father."

' "Child, for your lie and your shameful abuse of the sacredness of the confessional say four decades of the Rosary. It may be dark in here but I know who you are. If there is any reoccurrence of this blasphemous behaviour I will take the matter up with your father, so be warned."

' "Yes, Father." '

Elaine thought the incident in the confession-box was hilarious, but couldn't resist saying, 'That's not true!'

'Of course it's true. Half the church heard it.'

'Yeah,' said Gavin. 'You could hear Jake soon as he went

into the confession-box. Then the priest started.'

Jake looked daggers at his two so-called friends. He felt like telling them to ease up on the slagging. But he knew if it came to a battle of words he'd lose his temper and make himself look foolish in front of Elaine. He'd get his own back later.

'Want to hear another Jake story?' asked Gavin.

'Yes, please.'

'Ever hear of Bill Shankly?'

'Wasn't he the one who put Liverpool on the map?'

'Yeah. He was the manager who laid all the ground-work. Well, Jake went around Greystones telling everyone that Bill Shankly was comin' to watch him. That he was interested in signin' him for Liverpool.'

'Jake must be a very good player.'

'He couldn't kick snow off a rope.'

'Easy on, ' muttered Jake in an embarrassed undertone.

'That's for certain. He can't get his game with us, much less Liverpool.'

Suddenly Elaine realized there was something wrong with the story. 'Hey, Bill Shankly couldn't have come to watch Jake. He died years ago.'

'Well, that's Jake for you. It's bad enough telling lies . . . But coming up with one as obvious as that. What's left to say?'

'Don't believe them,' sulked Jake. 'None of it's true.'

'Course it's true. Ask anyone.'

Jake looked coldly at Gavin and Hammer. 'Come on, let's get out of here. You're supposed to be my friends. Have you anything good to say about anyone?'

The two lads shrugged and laughed. For the remainder of the run there wasn't a word spoken.

It was the last time Jake went for a run over Bray Head. And he kept out of Elaine's way for a while after that. Likewise he avoided Gavin and Hammer. With friends like that he'd go out and get himself a few enemies.

Although Mr Holmes had left Shamrock Boys, Luke never played football again. He built a makeshift loft and got friendly with some of the local pigeon fanciers. They gave him some surplus birds but none were quality pigeons and he knew in his heart that if he wanted to make proper progress he would have to come up with better stock. Often he used to cycle the Cliff Walk into Bray to the harbour, to see if there were any stray pigeons about, and sometimes he met the kids from the People's Park there. They told him that there were two pigeon clubs in Bray (there was none in Greystones) and if he ever wanted to race he would have to join one of them. He would also need a racing-clock, and a much better set up than he had in his loft in Greystones, not to mention better quality pigeons.

Luke began to save as much money as he could, working part-time on a newspaper round. He would have to raise the money to join a pigeon club, get a racing-clock, and buy some good quality stock-birds to breed off. All that would cost a fortune, especially the stock-birds – far too much for a fourteen-year-old. The birds were the biggest problem. The strays around the back of Bray Head which tired in the flight back to Dublin and the North of Ireland weren't the best to breed off. If they were top-class stock they wouldn't be forced down in a weak state; they would have been strong and resilient enough to stay in the sky until they got back home to their lofts.

No: if he wanted good stock he would have to wait until he had the money. There was no point in filling up the loft with rubbish. Quality, not quantity, was what he needed. But he also knew that when the summer races started he would cycle the Cliff Walk into Bray and pray that this would be the weekend, the day, the hour, the moment, when he would catch a top-class pigeon with his loop.

At least fifteen kids in Bray had the same wistful hope.

4

Two weeks after the friendly with Ballybrack, Shamrock Boys were drawn to play Riverside in the quarter-finals of the Cup. There were a few changes from the last meeting in the League. Lar Holmes was no longer manager. Luke was not playing. Neither was Chopper Doyle. He was still in the Riverside manager's bad books. The man just didn't want him in his car any more. Referee Harry Hennessy would also be an absentee. The only other difference was that the fixture was down for the Railway Field, not the People's Park in Bray.

Riverside planned to get to the Railway Field about fifteen minutes before kick-off time. Thirteen in all, including the manager, packed into the Opel estate on Bray's Dargle Road. Their football gear was packed outside on the roof-rack. Apart from being squashed Riverside boys were in fine fettle. They were out to give Shamrock Boys a stuffing. They were in fine form, having won all three of their previous League matches. They were shoving the top two teams all the way. And they had both teams at home right at the end of the season. They'd give them a walloping.

But for the present, they had their minds on the Cup. They sang and joked all the way from Bray to Greystones. They rolled down the windows of the Opel to give themselves extra room. Heads poked out of windows, arms too. They shouted comments to everyone they came across, especially going up the busy Main Street and through the traffic lights at the Town Hall.

'Hey, Mister, you dropped a fiver.'

'How's your belly for a lodger?'

'Hey, you. You don't look half as good as y'did last week on page three of the Sun.'

'Guard! Guard! Help us! We've been kidnapped!'n

'Stop it!' yelped the manager. 'I don't mind you shouting at people but not the Guards. It's against the law to carry more than five in a car.'

'Doesn't matter. Guards are too lazy to count. "Hiya, Guard, hiya. We're on a school tour. We're from St Joseph's School for Backward Boys. We're the school team an' we play backwards. See you, Guard."'

The Guard took the number of the car.

'He can write.'

'What?'

'He wrote down the number.'

'Now, look at the mess you got me into.'

Once past the Town Hall the traffic eased. Past the Vevay they were out into the country. The Opel pulled slowly up the steady gradient on the Bray side of Bray Head.

'Mr. Glynn, the car is goin' to stall.'

'No, it isn't.'

'Get out and push,' shouted another.

'Push! Push! Push!'

They were on the brow of Windgates. It was all downhill now. The hill was long and steep. It fell, fell, fell, into a hollow, and then up a short hill again before levelling off, past St Kevin's Boys School, and into Greystones.

Going down Windgates was like a roller-coaster ride. All shouts and whoops. All wind and speed. The car overshot the entrance to the Railway Field by a few yards. The brakes weren't too good. The Opel reversed and parked. Car doors opened. The hatch at the back opened. They untied their gear from the roof-rack and made a beeline for the pavilion. They rushed past the Shamrock Boys team without saying a word.

'I'm dyin' for a smoke.'

'I'm dyin' for a pee.'

43

'The gear got mixed up. I've two left-foot boots. Anyone got two right-foots?'

'Pity Chopper's not here. He could have thumped Gavin Byrne.'

'Mr Glynn, why's every team in the League got a dressing-room and we haven't?'

'Because we're a Third World team.'

'Are there no dressing-rooms in the Third Division?'

'Not Third Division, Third World. It means the poor, under-developed countries of the world. You know, the Third World.'

'No, I don't.'

'. . . Just forget it.'

'I'm starvin'. Anyone got an apple?'

'Mr Glynn, we can't have a second sub. There's only twelve players.'

'Where's Gerry?'

'He's visitin' his Da.'

'Where's his Da?'

'In jail.'

'What'd he do?'

'He went to work.'

'What does he work at? A burglar?'

'Nothin'. He was on the dole and got caught.'

Riverside were really hyped up. They were a good Cup team with a long tradition of success. Cup football suited them. It was hard and fast, and explosive. Something like themselves. It was real he-man stuff. They couldn't wait for the game to start. They had the bit between their teeth and couldn't wait to get stuck in.

And what was the girl doing on the side-line?

'See the girl on the side-line?'

'That's not a girl.'

'It is. She's too pretty to be a boy.'

'What's she doin' wearin' a track-suit?'

'Mr Glynn, they've a girl.'

'Where?'

'Over there.'

'She's surely not playing?'

'She's their coach. She's givin' a hand with the team.'

'How do you'know?'

'I asked one of their lads. He said she played in a friendly for them and they asked her to give a hand train the team.'

'I don't believe it. A girl coach. Anyway she's too young to coach. Get the referee's card.'

'What for?'

'See if her name is on it.'

'Why'd they put her name on it?'

'Maybe they're going to play her. Girls her age aren't allowed play in schoolboy leagues.'

'Doesn't matter. Let her play. They're goin' soft. They're ponces. We'll stuff them. We can beat girls, no bother.'

'Some girls are good players. Maybe if she's good they'll chance playing her.'

'Here's the referee's card. Her name's not on it.'

'Unless she's got a boy's name.'

'Or playin' in a boy's name.'

'Anyway who cares? We'll stuff them.'

The game kicked off. The Riverside Boys took the initiative from the start. Gavin was on song though. He was playing up front, making good use of what little possession he got. He was running straight at the Riverside defence. Soon they were at panic stations.

'We shoulda brought Chopper. Mr Glynn, I can't get near him. You shoulda brought Chopper.'

'Keep tight to him. Keep tight.'

'"I can't. I need some help.'

Riverside decided to put two men on Gavin.

On the side-line Elaine smiled. The extra marker would afford Shamrock Boys more freedom elsewhere. Hopefully in midfield.

Riverside were as busy as bees. They were playing short interpassing movements, moving neatly up the pitch. They knew there was no point in playing the ball through the middle for someone to run on to. Instead they played a lot of diagonal balls in the hope their wide players could latch on to them, and also pull the central defenders out of position. They knew that the through ball behind the central defenders wouldn't work as Hammer was very quick to turn (an ability almost unknown in centre-halves). When a ball was played in behind him he could turn and accelerate to a sprint from almost a standstill. He was always quicker off the mark than Gavin. Gavin could outsprint him over fifty to a hundred yards, but in a short sprint Hammer was unbeatable. And he could tackle. He had a bone-crusher of a tackle – hard but fair. In fact that was how he got his nickname.

Mousey Burke was getting overrun in midfield. He couldn't make an impact.

Elaine called for a substitution. 'Take off Mousey. Put on Joey Dunne.' Gerry Horgan, the new manager, agreed. 'Tell Gavin to drift wide and pull the two markers with him. That might leave the defence open and let Smyth in the back door.'

The manoeuvre nearly worked, but not quite. Robert had left his shooting boots at home. He got three clear-cut chances. Three times Gavin's markers fell for his ploy and drifted wide with him, leaving the openings for Robert to get into good scoring positions. Robert made a hash of all three opportunities.

Then Elaine called for another ploy. 'Tell Gavin to fall back deep, just in front of his own defence. See if the markers go with him.'

They didn't.

'Leave him there,' advised Elaine. 'He can take the odd run from deep midfield. They won't pick him up if he times his runs properly.'

46

Gavin picked his moment and ran from deep in the midfield. He surged from the back. It was like sauntering up a garden path. He took the ball right through and placed a sweet shot in the back of the Riverside net.

Riverside were stung. They didn't like it.

'Let me go forward, Mr. Glynn,' shouted the big Riverside centre-half.

'No, stay where you are.'

The centre-half went forward anyway and rattled a shot against the cross-bar.

'I'll rattle you next,' he shouted at Gummy Davis, the Shamrock Boys anchor-man in midfield. 'I'll put yer teeth down yer throat.'

'No, you won't.'

'Think not?'

'No. I left them in the dressing-room.'

Five minutes later Riverside scored a goal – a bullet-like drive from the centre-half. He saluted his manager and fell back into the defence, a contented smile on his face.

Half-time came and went. Still one-all. Rasher Murphy was getting daring. Either that, or he was showing off in front of Elaine. He was getting forward, overlapping, moving up along the flank in support. He went on a run. He beat the Riverside left-full on the outside. Then he brought the ball back, beat him on the inside and let fly with a scorcher that clipped off the outside of the goal-post.

Shortly after Rasher got caught out of position. The Riverside number 11 broke clear and sidefooted the ball into the Shamrock Boys net.

Panic stations.

The match plan was abandoned. Gavin came forward. Stayed forward. Even Hammer pushed up. They wanted an equalizer badly. And after that, a winner. Who in their right mind would want to play Riverside on their home patch in a Cup replay?

Time was running out. Riverside were feeling confident,

if not arrogant. They were slowing the game down, playing the ball towards the opposition's corner-flags and holding it there. It was looking like curtains for Shamrock Boys. They were on their way out of the Cup.

Then something controversial happened.

'Get on to the pitch.'

Gerry Horgan was telling Elaine to get out and play!

'But I can't. I'm not allowed to play. I'd be a protest.'

'You're a protest because you're a girl. Do y'call that fair?'

'No.'

'Well, get out there. To hell with them. John McLoughlin is on the card. Tell the ref you're J. McLoughlin.'

Elaine grabbed a jersey and got ready to go on. She stood at the half-way line waiting for a stoppage in play, so the referee could let her on to the pitch.

Eventually she got on. There were a few dark looks from the Riverside players and manager.

'What's your name?' asked the referee.

'J. McLoughlin,' answered Elaine.

'Ref, she's a girl.'

'That's nothing to do with me.'

'Ref, she's a girl. Girls aren't allowed to play.'

'How d'y'know she's a girl,' interrupted Rasher Murphy. 'Just 'cause she looks like one doesn't mean she is one. There's all kinds of things goin' nowadays.'

But the banter didn't matter, Elaine was on the pitch and that was that. She was told to work up front in tandem with Gavin, feeding off him. The idea was for her to get into scoring positions around the edge of the box. Hopefully it would be a classic situation between her and the Riverside goalkeeper. Gavin was to to draw the defence. It was up to Elaine to move into space and leave herself free to get in with a few shots at goal.

The pace became frantic. Robert Smyth threaded a ball through to Gavin. He turned his marker and squared the ball to Elaine. She dribbled past one defender. Then the big centre-half got ready to tackle her. He timed his tackle. Allowed her to get closer. Suddenly Elaine swerved, leaving the centre-half on the broad of his back. The goalkeeper hadn't an earthly. He tried to smother her well-directed shot. But he just couldn't get to it. It was out of reach. Elaine had scored the equalizer.

Almost in injury time Elaine was brought down in the penalty area. 'Macho-Man', the centre-half, was responsible. He went in with a rush of blood and a late tackle, and sent Elaine tumbling. He had tears in his eyes when the referee pointed to the penalty spot. Gavin took the kick.

G . . . O . . . A . . . L!

Almost from the tip-off the referee blew the full-time whistle. Shamrock Boys were in the semi-final of the Cup.

'We was done,' moaned 'Macho-Man'. 'We was done. Done by a team of pansies.'

Two days later there was a protest against Elaine Clarke. But Riverside couldn't prove their case. It was something similar to the Chopper Doyle protest a few weeks earlier in the People's Park. Nobody could prove that J. McLoughlin was not John McLoughlin, as listed on the referee's card. Riverside, apart from hearsay, couldn't prove that J. McLoughlin was a girl. The protest was thrown out. But, privately, the League committee took note of Elaine Clarke's name.

Riverside were furious. Things went mute for a while down by the Dargle side and in the back of Mr Glynn's Opel estate. But as far as the Shamrock Boys were concerned the glory days were in full swing at the Railway Field. They were out of the running for the League title but they felt that they had a good chance of winning the Cup.

Even Lar Holmes was delighted with their upswing in fortune.

Those were the days, my friend. Those were the days.

Around this time Jake got to know a cool dude whom the local kids called Mike the Shaker. He was English and used to play with a top rock group until they broke up. He had come to live incognito in Greystones, but all the kids knew who he really was. He was full of hair; hair all over his face. You could hardly see his nose. Jake got to know him and they struck up a friendship. They spent a lot of time together and Mike taught Jake to play the guitar real cool dude style. Jake was a natural as far as music was concerned. He only had to hear a tune once and he could play it straight back. He had a great ear for music.

Mike and Jake were to spend a lot of time together. Jake even disappeared from around the team for a while. But their friendship wouldn't last for ever. Mike was a restless soul and somewhere along the line he was bound to get the urge to move on. Some day soon he would sit down and have a rethink on his life. He'd sort his situation out. Maybe get his hair cut and rediscover himself. Then go back to England to the rock scene. But before he'd go he'd leave Jake a finer and wiser musician.

Mike was a great tutor and Jake would learn to the full.

Shamrock Boys made it all the way to the U-14 Cup Final.

Elaine played in the semi-final, this time in her own name. The opposition, Rathnew, didn't protest. They didn't think it fair to object. After all she was the right age group and played solely for Shamrock Boys. But the League committee notified Shamrock Boys that they were not to play her in the final.

When he heard of the League's directive, Lar Holmes went bananas. He had been impressed with Elaine. As he wasn't involved with a football club any more he rang the League secretary and gave free vent to his disgust.

'You've no right to treat her like that.'

'She can't play. The rules are the rules.'

'It's discrimination.'

'Rules are rules. We go by the rules.'

'I'll give you rules. I'll give you free publicity in every newspaper in the country. I'll give you rules. I'll have every Women's Rights organization at your front door.'

'It's all been tried before, Lar, and failed.'

'I won't give you Irish law. I'll give you European law.'

'What d'you mean by that, Lar?'

'I'll give you the European Court on Human Rights. Your League is supposed to foster underage soccer. Your League discriminates against girls.'

'We don't discriminate against girls.'

'Why don't you let them play then?'

'We've changed the rules. We allow girls to play up to U-12 level. There's girls' leagues elsewhere that cater for girls over our age limit.'

'Yes, in Dublin. This isn't Dublin. Why don't you set up a league locally? You just couldn't be bothered. You just don't want to know.'

'No need to get shirty, Lar.'

'I'm not getting shirty. But you will. Before all this is over you'll be sorry you ever heard of Elaine Clarke, or me for that matter.'

'Let's talk this over, Lar.'

'There's no talking it over. The only ones you'll be talking it over with will be the Employment Equality Agency. You can have a proper oul' barney.'

'Just because you got hassle from Shamrock Boys . . .'

'I got no hassle from Shamrock Boys.'

'They put you out, didn't they?'

'Have it your way. But this one's from the heart.'

Lar Holmes put the phone down. At least, he'd make the League sweat. He didn't want revenge. He only wanted justice. Justice for Elaine Clarke.

Gavin and Hammer found out about Lar Holmes's phone-call to the League secretary shortly afterwards. They had just come back with Elaine after a run over Bray Head. They were standing outside her house when Mrs Clarke came out of the front door, fuming. She spoke to Elaine.

'I've just had a phone-call from someone representing the football league you played a few matches in.'

Elaine looked to Hammer and Gavin. 'Trouble?'

'Elaine, you're not to play any more matches in that league.'

'He wasn't giving out, Mum, was he? I only played two matches anyway.'

'No, *he* wasn't giving out but I was. He would hardly listen to me. He went on and on about some man who has threatened to organize a protest campaign on account of you not being allowed play in the boys' soccer league.'

Hammer laughed. 'That'll be cool, Elaine. You'll be all over the papers.'

Elaine's mother gave Hammer a cutting glance. 'That's precisely what I don't want. I don't want Elaine's name to be used . . . because that's all it will be . . . she will only be used. I don't want this thing turned into a circus with newspaper people banging our front door down. The gall of the man.'

Gavin was getting curious. 'Did he say who was goin' to organize the protest?'

Mrs Clarke didn't seem to have heard him. She went on, 'I told him that I didn't give two hoots . . . that Elaine wasn't playing any more football . . . that she would be involved in athletics instead . . . I told him that football was full of male chauvinists . . .'

'You didn't, Mum!'

'I did.'

'Who did he say was goin' to organize the protest, Mrs Clarke?'

'I told him in no uncertain terms. He said that they'd had this kind of trouble before. That the issue went through the courts – that the courts found that the school-

52

boy football authorities had no case to answer. And listen to this . . . that as a concession the league had decided to allow girls up to the age of twelve play in their league, but not over that. Big deal! That sickened me . . . really made me mad.

'I told him where to go with his league, that my daughter couldn't be bothered playing in it . . . I told him . . . I told him to tell this Lar Holmes fellow to forget about organizing a protest . . . that over my dead body he'd organize a protest . . .'

At the mention of Lar Holmes's name both Gavin and Hammer laughed. But not for long. Only for as long as it took Mrs Clarke to focus a withering glare at them.

'Stop sniggering. Do you know this Lar Holmes?'

'Mum, he used to . . .'

'I'm not asking you. I'm asking them.'

'Course we know him, Mrs Clarke. He used to be our football manager.'

'A troublemaker?'

'No. But he'd champion a lost cause.'

'Well he's lost his cause already. I told the league fellow to tell Lar Holmes that we don't want this matter taken any further. If it is, Mr Holmes will be receiving a solicitor's letter. That, hopefully, will stop him in his tracks and put an end to all this ridiculous hullabaloo . . . Elaine, five minutes. Then be inside; you've some work to do.'

Mrs Clarke turned on her heel and went back into the house. Her temper, as yet, hadn't subsided.

Elaine began to laugh. Then Gavin, and finally Hammer. They couldn't help it. It was infectious. But it was just as well Mrs Clarke didn't see them.

Within a day or two the storm would blow over and the world would be at peace.

5

The U-14 Cup Final was played in Bray on the first Sunday in June. The League title was already settled. Arklow had won it, with Riverside finishing second, one point behind. The Cup Final was between Shamrock Boys and Arklow.

The furore over Elaine playing in the League had just about died down. She had seen Lar Holmes and asked him to forget about setting up a protest campaign on her behalf. At first he was reluctant. But when she told him she was giving up football to concentrate on athletics he softened. This, allied to the fact that Elaine's parents didn't want the nuisance of the publicity and ill-feeling that was sure to follow such a heavily orchestrated campaign, made Lar Holmes abandon his crusade for equal rights on Elaine's behalf.

The Cup Final in Bray was to be Elaine's last game giving a hand with the team. She had decided to make a clean break. Once the Cup Final was over she'd cut away from football altogether. All her sporting efforts from then on would concentrate on her athletics career.

The lads knew they wouldn't see much of her again. She came from a different social background and once contact through football was lost, she would more than likely go out of their lives. Add the fact that Elaine went to school in Bray and as her friends were from there she would spend most of her free time socializing in Bray, which meant that they wouldn't even see her around Greystones. She had moved among them, but once the Cup Final was over they would lose all contact with her.

Shamrock Boys and Arklow had a lot of support for the Cup Final. Arklow had even brought a pipe-band. They intended marching behind the band before the kick-off. It had even been suggested that there be a victory parade through Bray's Main Street after the match – and they could see themselves leading it. But they were wary of Shamrock Boys, Gavin in particular. They just weren't confident of containing him.

The two teams had met the week before in Arklow in a back League match. Arklow only needed a draw to win the League. Their confidence in containing Gavin was so fragile that they let the grass grow a little bit longer in the hope it would slow the Shamrock Boys' striker down.

'Why did you let the grass grow so long?'

'Sure ye know how it is. This time a year the grass grows overnight.'

'I think your players grow overnight, too. Why didn't you cut the grass before the match?'

'Sure the mower broke.'

'You could have hired another.'

'Sure we could. But the shop that hires them out went bankrupt.'

'There's no fear of you goin' bankrupt, you crafty oul' codger.'

'Now, don't be talkin' like that. Sure it's only a game of sport. And aren't we only doin' it for the chaps?'

Arklow were a country team. And their manager was a country fellow. But there were no flies on either him or the team. They knew the game inside out. And the grass ploy worked. Arklow won the match, and the League.

Not only was the Cup Final to be Elaine's last contact with Shamrock Boys, it was to be Gavin's last game as well. At the time nobody knew this, not even Gavin. But several teams in the Dublin Schoolboys League knew of him and were interested in signing him. After today, Gavin would never again tog out for Shamrock Boys.

But first there was the important matter of settling the issue of a U-14 Cup Final.

Elaine and Gerry Horgan had discussed the tactics for the game the night before. In the dressing-rooms, just before the match, they relayed those tactics to the players:

'4-3-3. Usual back four. Usual midfield, except one less with Mousey moving up front to play wide on the flanks. He can use both feet. That means he can play as a winger on either side of the park. Mousey, stay wide and bring the ball to the end-line. That'll beat the off-side trap. Send the ball across, on to the far post. Gavin, be there. Robert, stay sharp. Keep as far forward as possible. And *move*; no standing around. Got me?'

'Gotcha.'

'Midfield's very important. That's where Arklow is strongest. Don't let them move midfield. Stifle them. Pick them up quick and hard. Don't let them play the ball. Pick them up tight.'

'Yeah.'

'The fulls, don't let nobody take you on the inside. Keep them on the outside. Out as near the touch-line as possible. Hammer . . .'

'What?'

'You take the free kicks from the back and just inside their half. Anything direct, twenty yards or so, let Gavin take. Bend them. Shoot for goal. Rasher . . .'

'Wha?'

'Don't go too far forward. Not unless you're covered. And don't end up in Arklow's penalty area whatever you do. We can't afford to leave the back open. Mousey, take the corners. Outswingers, out of the goalkeeper's reach. And one last thing: Under no circumstances get caught in possession. Lay the ball off neatly. Play it around. Twenty yards out, shoot. Get plenty of shots in. No trying to walk the ball into the net. The first fifteen minutes build from the back. Take it cool. Settle. Right, get out there and do the business.'

Shamrock Boys lined up in the corridor beside Arklow.

They had to wait until the match officials came out of their dressing-room to check the players' studs, etc. Outside they could hear the pipe-band playing. It was rousing stuff. Good job they weren't playing against Chopper Doyle and company.

Rasher passed a remark about the pipe-band. 'We shoulda taken our porridge this mornin'. This is all Scottish Highlands stuff.'

The match officials came into the corridor, with Harry Hennessy. Luckily he was only doing the line.

The referee checked both teams' studs. The referee's card, with both teams' names listed, was handed to him.

The match officials led the way out to the pitch. There was a cheer from the two hundred or so supporters. Most of them were family (Gavin and Hammer's parents, sisters and brothers included), fellow club associates, and the players and officials of some of the local clubs.

As they paraded around the pitch behind the pipe-band, they could see Jake sitting behind the top goal holding audience with a group of nine-year-olds. He was wearing a gigantic Shamrock Boys scarf and a Mexican sombrero. He was busy telling the kids yarns – fabrications of tall stories and even taller stories.

Lar Holmes was there too, lost in the crowd.

Just over from Jake, Chopper Doyle was hosting a card-school. He looked up as the parade turned by the corner-flag. He gave a discontented look and quickly delved back into the card-game. Jake shouted over to him, 'How'ya, Chopper? Hear you're takin' drivin' lessons.'

'Yeah, in the squad-car.'

The pre-match parade finished at the centre-circle. There it came to a standstill. The pipe-band played the National Anthem.

The respective management teams kept to opposite sides, though the Arklow manager refused to stay in his dug-out. He paced the side-line for the duration of the game. He was a half-manager, half-fan, a total damned nuisance.

Shamrock Boys won the toss. They took choice of ends. Arklow kicked off. Immediately there was a roar from the Arklow manager, followed by another roar. He never shut up the whole first half.

The crowd were busy at it too, especially when the play approached the respective penalty areas. It was real end-to-end stuff. But it was obvious to all the neutral fans present that Gavin and Hammer were a cut above the other players. They were more decisive and more skilful. They oozed confidence and class.

As a matter of interest, the referee wasn't bad. He was fair. He seemed to have a favourite phrase though: 'Play on! Play on!' He made good use of the advantage rule. And he let the game flow as much as possible without being over-restrictive with the whistle.

'Play on!'

The Arklow outside-left began to titter to his nearest team-mate, 'Guess what he'll say next?'

'Play on!'

And 'Play on!' it was.

The first half ended scoreless. Mousey Burke had a shot taken off the line. The Arklow centre-forward missed two golden opportunities. On the second, he overplayed the ball, and Hammer came out of nowhere, and took it off his boot with as crisp a tackle as could be perfected.

The referee blew for half-time.

The teams withdrew to the dressing-rooms for the half-time break. The pipe-band came on to the pitch.

Fifteen minutes later the two teams were back out on the pitch for the second half.

Within minutes Arklow scored a fluke. The Arklow manager became ecstatic. He danced up and down the side-line. Then quietened.

All of a sudden things just wouldn't go right for Shamrock Boys. The ball wouldn't run for them. Fifty-fifty balls, everything seemed to break for Arklow. It just wasn't going to be Shamrock Boys' day.

Gavin got the ball eighteen yards out. It was a dropping ball. He volleyed it with the outside of his foot. It curled straight for the top corner. Thump! The ball twanged off the angle of the cross-bar.

Robert Smyth latched on to the rebound. He hit it first time. The ball struck the bottom of the far upright and spun back into play, but Gummy Davis was beaten to it by the despairing dive of the Arklow goalkeeper. The ball just wouldn't go in.

With fifteen minutes to go Shamrock Boys' rhythm was broken by a flare-up between the referee and the Arklow number 6.

The referee proceeded to book him for a foul.

'What's your name?'

'Roy Rogers.'

'Say that again.'

'Roy Rogers. You don't believe me?'

'No.'

'Well, ask me manager.'

The referee went over to the Arklow manager.

'What's his name?'

'Roy Rogers.'

The referee went back to the player. He took out the referee's card and checked it. 'Roy Rogers' was listed.

'Now don't tell me you have a horse and its name is Trigger.'

'No, I've a goat, though.'

'What?'

'A pet goat – called Harry, after Harry Hennessy.'

The referee scowled and cautioned him. The game restarted. It took an additional ten minutes for Shamrock Boys to regain their momentum, but not before Arklow scored a second goal.

On the side-line, Elaine knew it was a lost cause. Arklow's name was destined to be on the Cup.

The final whistle went. The Cup Final was over. Shamrock Boys had lost. Arklow were jubilant.

On the victory parade up Bray Main Street the Arklow manager said to a *Wicklow People* reporter, 'Sure, for every winner there has to be a loser. And if it wasn't for the losers there'd be no Cup competition. Sure, isn't it great. I just knew we 'd win. If I'd known we'd lose sure I wouldn't have brought the pipe-band.'

> End of season.
> End of Elaine playing soccer.
> End of Gavin playing for Shamrock Boys.

About the start of July, a few weeks after Shamrock Boys played in the U-14 Cup Final, Luke cycled the Cliff Walk to Bray harbour to see if there were any stray pigeons about.

It was a Saturday evening, about seven o'clock. He hadn't seen much on Bray Head.

There were several flocks flying over but no birds were coming down. They were all flying resolutely on towards Dublin and the North of Ireland.

In Bray harbour the situation was a lot better. There were some pigeons down in twos and threes. There were plenty of kids about, with pigeon loops laid out, trying to entice the hungry pigeons with grains of pigeon corn.

To the left of the quayside there were a few factory units. They mostly had flat roofs. Some of the pigeons circling over the harbour used the roofs as a vantage-point before gliding on to the quayside. As it was a Saturday night and the factories were closed some kids got up on the roofs, got their loops ready and sprinkled some pigeon corn.

'Don't go up on that part,' someone advised Luke.

'Why not?'

'It's asbestos. See where it's patched up?'

'There?'

'That's where Tony Healy fell through a few weeks ago.'

'Did he hurt himself?'

'Concussed and broke his arm. The ambulance had to come and take him away. There's murder over it. The security man keeps comin' in his car and tellin' us to keep off the roofs. If you see a car comin' get down quick.'

Some of the kids had cardboard boxes with them. They kept them out of view just inside the boundary wall between the quayside and the factories. Every so often a pigeon was looped and stored in one of the cardboard boxes until it was time to go home.

Luke had brought a cardboard box with him on the back-carrier of his bike. He left it propped up against the boundary wall. He had his eye on a blue chequer hen. He got down off the roof, set his loop and sprinkled a trail of corn both inside and outside the loop. The hen was making steady progress picking at the corn. Luke waited a minute or so, then made his way over to the long arm of the loop. All of a sudden he bent down to pull it. But the bird fluttered up and landed a few feet further down the quayside.

Luke recommenced his vigil. He was successful this time and caught the hen. It had a GB racing ring. He put it into the cardboard box and set up again, this time on the far side of the harbour bridge. There was too much movement going on where he had just been. Things were a lot quieter on the far side of the bridge. The pigeons wouldn't be as easily frightened. They would be more at ease and that little bit easier to catch. He caught a second bird, a pied cock.

A man was standing on the bridge. Luke wasn't certain whether he was watching the lads trying to catch pigeons or using it as an excuse to see if there were any salmon passing under the bridge from the sea into the mouth of the Dargle river. Perhaps he was doing both. Anyway, it was a nice way of passing a summer's evening, with the bonus of all the activity among the boating fraternity.

The man went over to Luke.

'You Peter Lynch's son from Greystones?'

'Yes, I am.'

'You're a dead ringer for the oul' man. I used to work with him. How's he keepin'?'

'Well.'

'Workin', is he?'

'Doin' a bit.'

'Got many pigeons?'

'Just a few.'

'Intend racin'?'

'Sometime, I hope.'

'Know much about them?'

'Not a lot.'

'I keep pigeons myself. I could teach you a thing or two about them. Pretty soon I might have to give them up. The doctor's been warnin' me off. The oul' lungs an' that. I think the Doc is givin' me until the end of August to get rid of the pigeons. He's serious this time. He'll make me do it. If I can't get out of it I'll keep a few back for you. Have you got a decent loft?'

'No, just a kind of a one.'

'Well, build a good loft. I don't want my birds goin' to some oul' kip. Build a decent loft an' I promise you a few good birds. An' that's a deal.'

'Sure.'

'Tell your father Des Keogh was askin' for him. See you the end of August.'

The man went off, walked off towards the Harbour Bar, turned right, and headed up the hill towards the Seapoint Road and the bridge at the bottom of the town.

Luke hung around the harbour for a further two hours. Then he got back on the bike and pedalled along the Promenade towards the Cliff Walk and the five-mile cycle home.

ll, Larry did a lot for us. Runnin' around after us.
in' money out of his own pocket. He put a lot of
in. And there he was for the last year with no job,
e were only laughin' and abusin' him. It makes you
. . . Hammer, Elaine was right when she told you to
Shamrock Boys. She was right. We should make use
 talent. We should try to get on. Look at poor Lar
es. Look at your father. Look at my father.'
at's wrong with our fathers?'
thing. They're just broken-down builders' labourers,
all.'
at are you tryin' to say?'
 tryin' to say that through football we could get on in
'e could do things our fathers never did.'
akes more than dreamin' to make it in football. For
t never happens.'
mmer, know what your problem is?'
at?'
're too damned downbeat.'
t's your opinion.'
ll, I'm not goin' to end up like Lar Holmes – no job
 a mental home. I'm goin' to do something with my
nd I'm startin' now. Next season I'm not playin' for
rock Boys, and that's that.'
laine felt like smiling, she was careful not to let it

t any offers?'
, but I'll put word out, and the offers won't be long
nin' in.'
e lads won't like you for that.'
 hell with the lads. They don't care about the team.
re only a crowd of messers.'
he last few minutes all three – Gavin, Hammer and
 – had come to a standstill. Gavin and Hammer
 facing one another. A row was brewing. Elaine
ed in between them.

He wondered if the man would keep his promise and
give him some pigeons.

That wasn't the only thing he wondered. He wondered
if the pigeons would be any good, or only rubbish.

Jake was on a talent-spotting mission. Word went around
Greystones that he intended to form a rock group.

He held auditions in one of the shelters on the south
beach.

Three musicians showed up.

One had a tin whistle.

'Where did you learn to play that?'

'The Christian Brothers.'

Another had an accordian.

'Where did you get that?'

'The School for the Blind.'

The third had a fiddle.

'This,' said Jake, 'is an audition for a rock group, not a
céilí band.'

The failed applicants went home disappointed, but not
as disappointed as Jake. When he got home he discovered
that his mother had cleared out his room and thrown his
sheets of lyrics into the dustbin.

He went outside and found the dustbin was already
emptied. He tracked the lorry down.

'You've got my songs.'

'Your what?'

'My music.'

'Who do you think you are, John Lennon?'

Jake said nothing; just followed the lorry to the dump
and got his songs back.

He had learned two lessons:

1. Hide your songs from your mother;

2. Never attempt to recruit a rock band in Greystones.

6

Hammer was surprised to get a phone-call from Elaine early one morning during the summer holidays. None of the lads had heard from her for over a month.

'Coming for a run?' she asked.

'We didn't think we'd hear from you again.'

'Why? Did you think I'd gone away?'

'No. Seein' you're finished with football, we thought you'd be finished with us.'

'No, we can always go for a run together. We can keep in touch that way.'

'How are the athletics goin'?'

'Going very well. I'm doing a lot of speed training. I need a bit of a change. That's why I want to go for a run over Bray Head and the Cliff Walk.'

'Winnin' many races?'

'A few. Though it's tough. I'm running against much older girls. But I'm working on it.'

And Elaine *was* working on it. She was having trouble getting up to the best times she had set in England. The winter lay off had affected her form. But now that she was settling in with Crusaders she would train flat out during the winter and be well-prepared for the new track season. She should have regained her personal best by then and be setting new times, new standards.

'See you in an hour at the back of the Amusement Arcade, just where the gate leads on to the path for the Cliff Walk. And, if you can, bring Gavin with you. We can have a good chat as we run.'

Hammer got in touch with Gavin.

Gavin was surprised to hear that Elaine wanted to go for a

run with them. 'I always thought she was a [...] said. 'But maybe she's not. I really thought sh[...]

'She's not a snob. It's her accent. Think sh[...] with us if she was a snob? Not likely!'

Elaine was waiting at the entrance to the [...]

'How's it goin'?'

'Great.'

'Glad to see you, Elaine.'

They jogged along the path, wanting to v[...] It was flat for the first mile, with fields to th[...] and the sea on the right. Straight ahead to[...] of Bray Head. Gradually the flat of the fi[...] the beach was railed by cliffs. The path i[...] steepened. They were on the first part [...] Walk. The path narrowed with bushes and [...] both sides. They were beginning to feel a sl[...]

'Suppose you heard about Lar Holmes[...] Elaine.

'No. What about him?'

'His mind snapped. They say it was be[...] job.'

Hammer shrugged. 'You never know [...] They say he hadn't worked in over a yea[...] thing was playing on his mind. And the[...] out about him being a crank.'

'That's sad. I must pay him a visit.'

'Elaine, he's in the looney-bin.'

'Don't say that! Lots of people have [...] downs.'

'They took him away in case he'd be [...] self.'

'You know,' said Gavin, 'it's only w[...] things like that that it makes you think.'

'Think of what?'

'Hammer, don't be so thick.'

'I'm not being thick. It makes you think[...]

'Why don't you have a talk with my father,' she suggested.

'What's your father got to do with it?'

'He played for and coached Coventry City. He might be able to give you some advice.'

'We don't want advice,' cursed Hammer.

'Don't mind him. I want advice. Maybe he doesn't. But I want it.'

'Come down to the house some night and see him. He won't mind. He was something like yourselves. His parents weren't well-to-do. He went to England as an apprentice and slogged it out. There wasn't much money in the game in those days. But he made a name for himself as a footballer and it stood to him. He was lucky. A lot of others made nothing. They ended up broke. Why don't you have a word with him?'

'Maybe we will.'

'Well, I will,' said Gavin.

They continued with the run, turning left up on to the track which led to the top of Bray Head. By the time they got down into the wood on the far side everything was calm again.

They went through the wood, then on to the path where the Cliff Walk began in Bray.

There Hammer had a change of heart. 'I think I'll go with you to hear what Elaine's father has to say. But one thing . . .'

'What?'

'I'm not leavin' Shamrock Boys as long as there's a team. I'll only leave if the team breaks up.'

They got back to Greystones half an hour later.

The following Tuesday night Gavin and Hammer went to see Elaine's father. When they knocked on the door Elaine answered. She winked, and brought them into the sitting-room to her father. Having introduced them, she left. 'Back in a few minutes,' she said.

Mr Clarke looked older than the boys imagined he would. He had quit football altogether and come back to Ireland to live. Elaine said he worked for some big company. It wasn't a great job but it kept him going.

'Enjoying your football?' he asked.

'Yes.'

'That helps . . . Elaine says you could do with some advice. Well, first thing you should do about advice is – listen! It takes nothing out of you. If you don't like what you hear, let it go in one ear and out the other. But if you think it makes sense, take note.

'Which of you is Hammer?'

'I am.'

'Elaine tells me you don't want to leave Shamrock Boys. Well, think again. I don't accept that it should be on your conscience if you left. You owe Shamrock Boys nothing. Once the season is over and the fixture list is completed, that's that.

'Next season is important for both of you. U-15 matters. Tell me why it matters?'

'U-15 is representative football.'

'Yes, you can play schoolboy international at that age, and if you reach schoolboy international standard you come under the attention of the cross-channel scouts. That's why it's important. It's the start of the screening process for a career in professional football. The key to that door is very good footballing ability *and* the necessary drive to succeed.'

'But ability and drive are not all,' Mr Clarke went on. 'If you want to get to the top, be with a big club. Joining a bigger club won't make you a better player – good players are born, not made – but it will give you the opportunity to get on. Big clubs have clout. If you're with one you get noticed – most selection committees, and even club scouts, have the attitude that by fifteen all the top players are

He wondered if the man would keep his promise and give him some pigeons.

That wasn't the only thing he wondered. He wondered if the pigeons would be any good, or only rubbish.

Jake was on a talent-spotting mission. Word went around Greystones that he intended to form a rock group.

He held auditions in one of the shelters on the south beach.

Three musicians showed up.

One had a tin whistle.

'Where did you learn to play that?'

'The Christian Brothers.'

Another had an accordian.

'Where did you get that?'

'The School for the Blind.'

The third had a fiddle.

'This,' said Jake, 'is an audition for a rock group, not a *céilí* band.'

The failed applicants went home disappointed, but not as disappointed as Jake. When he got home he discovered that his mother had cleared out his room and thrown his sheets of lyrics into the dustbin.

He went outside and found the dustbin was already emptied. He tracked the lorry down.

'You've got my songs.'

'Your what?'

'My music.'

'Who do you think you are, John Lennon?'

Jake said nothing; just followed the lorry to the dump and got his songs back.

He had learned two lessons:

1. Hide your songs from your mother;
2. Never attempt to recruit a rock band in Greystones.

6

Hammer was surprised to get a phone-call from Elaine early one morning during the summer holidays. None of the lads had heard from her for over a month.

'Coming for a run?' she asked.

'We didn't think we'd hear from you again.'

'Why? Did you think I'd gone away?'

'No. Seein' you're finished with football, we thought you'd be finished with us.'

'No, we can always go for a run together. We can keep in touch that way.'

'How are the athletics goin'?'

'Going very well. I'm doing a lot of speed training. I need a bit of a change. That's why I want to go for a run over Bray Head and the Cliff Walk.'

'Winnin' many races?'

'A few. Though it's tough. I'm running against much older girls. But I'm working on it.'

And Elaine *was* working on it. She was having trouble getting up to the best times she had set in England. The winter lay off had affected her form. But now that she was settling in with Crusaders she would train flat out during the winter and be well-prepared for the new track season. She should have regained her personal best by then and be setting new times, new standards.

'See you in an hour at the back of the Amusement Arcade, just where the gate leads on to the path for the Cliff Walk. And, if you can, bring Gavin with you. We can have a good chat as we run.'

Hammer got in touch with Gavin.

Gavin was surprised to hear that Elaine wanted to go for a

run with them. 'I always thought she was a bit of a snob,' he said. 'But maybe she's not. I really thought she'd blown us.'

'She's not a snob. It's her accent. Think she'd go for a run with us if she was a snob? Not likely!'

Elaine was waiting at the entrance to the path.

'How's it goin'?'

'Great.'

'Glad to see you, Elaine.'

They jogged along the path, wanting to warm up slowly. It was flat for the first mile, with fields to the left, the beach and the sea on the right. Straight ahead towered the back of Bray Head. Gradually the flat of the fields sloped and the beach was railed by cliffs. The path in front of them steepened. They were on the first part of the real Cliff Walk. The path narrowed with bushes and wild growth on both sides. They were beginning to feel a slight strain.

'Suppose you heard about Lar Holmes?' said Gavin to Elaine.

'No. What about him?'

'His mind snapped. They say it was because he lost his job.'

Hammer shrugged. 'You never know what's goin' on. They say he hadn't worked in over a year. That the whole thing was playing on his mind. And there was us givin' out about him being a crank.'

'That's sad. I must pay him a visit.'

'Elaine, he's in the looney-bin.'

'Don't say that! Lots of people have nervous breakdowns.'

'They took him away in case he'd be a danger to himself.'

'You know,' said Gavin, 'it's only when you hear of things like that that it makes you think.'

'Think of what?'

'Hammer, don't be so thick.'

'I'm not being thick. It makes you think of what?'

'Well, Larry did a lot for us. Runnin' around after us. Spendin' money out of his own pocket. He put a lot of effort in. And there he was for the last year with no job, and we were only laughin' and abusin' him. It makes you think. . . . Hammer, Elaine was right when she told you to leave Shamrock Boys. She was right. We should make use of our talent. We should try to get on. Look at poor Lar Holmes. Look at your father. Look at my father.'

'What's wrong with our fathers?'

'Nothing. They're just broken-down builders' labourers, that's all.'

'What are you tryin' to say?'

'I'm tryin' to say that through football we could get on in life. We could do things our fathers never did.'

'It takes more than dreamin' to make it in football. For most it never happens.'

'Hammer, know what your problem is?'

'What?'

'You're too damned downbeat.'

'That's your opinion.'

'Well, I'm not goin' to end up like Lar Holmes – no job and in a mental home. I'm goin' to do something with my life. And I'm startin' now. Next season I'm not playin' for Shamrock Boys, and that's that.'

If Elaine felt like smiling, she was careful not to let it show.

'Got any offers?'

'No, but I'll put word out, and the offers won't be long in comin' in.'

'The lads won't like you for that.'

'To hell with the lads. They don't care about the team. They're only a crowd of messers.'

In the last few minutes all three – Gavin, Hammer and Elaine – had come to a standstill. Gavin and Hammer stood facing one another. A row was brewing. Elaine stepped in between them.

'Why don't you have a talk with my father,' she suggested.

'What's your father got to do with it?'

'He played for and coached Coventry City. He might be able to give you some advice.'

'We don't want advice,' cursed Hammer.

'Don't mind him. I want advice. Maybe he doesn't. But I want it.'

'Come down to the house some night and see him. He won't mind. He was something like yourselves. His parents weren't well-to-do. He went to England as an apprentice and slogged it out. There wasn't much money in the game in those days. But he made a name for himself as a footballer and it stood to him. He was lucky. A lot of others made nothing. They ended up broke. Why don't you have a word with him?'

'Maybe we will.'

'Well, I will,' said Gavin.

They continued with the run, turning left up on to the track which led to the top of Bray Head. By the time they got down into the wood on the far side everything was calm again.

They went through the wood, then on to the path where the Cliff Walk began in Bray.

There Hammer had a change of heart. 'I think I'll go with you to hear what Elaine's father has to say. But one thing . . .'

'What?'

'I'm not leavin' Shamrock Boys as long as there's a team. I'll only leave if the team breaks up.'

They got back to Greystones half an hour later.

The following Tuesday night Gavin and Hammer went to see Elaine's father. When they knocked on the door Elaine answered. She winked, and brought them into the sitting-room to her father. Having introduced them, she left. 'Back

in a few minutes,' she said.

Mr Clarke looked older than the boys imagined he would. He had quit football altogether and come back to Ireland to live. Elaine said he worked for some big company. It wasn't a great job but it kept him going.

'Enjoying your football?' he asked.

'Yes.'

'That helps . . . Elaine says you could do with some advice. Well, first thing you should do about advice is – listen! It takes nothing out of you. If you don't like what you hear, let it go in one ear and out the other. But if you think it makes sense, take note.

'Which of you is Hammer?'

'I am.'

'Elaine tells me you don't want to leave Shamrock Boys. Well, think again. I don't accept that it should be on your conscience if you left. You owe Shamrock Boys nothing. Once the season is over and the fixture list is completed, that's that.

'Next season is important for both of you. U-15 matters. Tell me why it matters?'

'U-15 is representative football.'

'Yes, you can play schoolboy international at that age, and if you reach schoolboy international standard you come under the attention of the cross-channel scouts. That's why it's important. It's the start of the screening process for a career in professional football. The key to that door is very good footballing ability *and* the necessary drive to succeed.'

'But ability and drive are not all,' Mr Clarke went on. 'If you want to get to the top, be with a big club. Joining a bigger club won't make you a better player – good players are born, not made – but it will give you the opportunity to get on. Big clubs have clout. If you're with one you get noticed – most selection committees, and even club scouts, have the attitude that by fifteen all the top players are

playing for the top clubs. A small club like Shamrock Boys nobody wants to know. Except maybe one of the big boys who's out to poach a player. The Dublin Schoolboys League is the league to be in – and playing for one of their top club teams at that.

'Regarding England that's another day's talk. You have to take matters step by step. If you ever get the opportunity to play English League football come back and I'll give you my tuppence worth.'

Mr Clarke looked over at the glass cabinet in the corner of the room. It was full of trophies that Elaine had won in England. But at the front there were three tasselled caps and a gold medal in a presentation box.

'Know what they are?' Mr Clarke asked, pointing.

'Irish international caps.'

'Dead right. And know what this is?' he said, sliding open the glass cabinet and taking out the gold medal.

'A Cup-winner's medal?'

'An FA Cup-winner's medal. Every English League professional's ambition.' Mr Clarke turned and put the medal back in the cabinet. 'Remember that you need ability, drive and determination to succeed.' He turned and looked Hammer full square in the face . . . 'Ability alone is not enough. It's just the tip of the iceberg.'

Hammer felt uneasy. He looked away from Mr Clarke's searching gaze.

Gavin just smiled. The man was right.

Elaine came into the room with her mother. The lads felt uneasy. Mrs Clarke asked them if they would like a cup of tea or coffee.

'No, thanks. We'd better be going.'

'Don't be in such a hurry.'

'All right. Okay. We'd like a cup of coffee.'

They didn't leave the house until 10.30.

As they found out, the Clarkes were real chatter-boxes. All three of them

69

Apart from promising Luke a few pigeons, Des Keogh, the man whom Luke had met at the harbour in Bray, also passed on some much needed advice on how to bring pigeons into top condition for the various distance races. Usually fanciers never passed on the secrets of their success, not while they were still in competition, so Luke was lucky to come across someone who was prepared to coach him, in the finer points of breeding and training winning pigeons. None of Des Keogh's birds were top race winners, but they were near enough, and Luke hoped to cross-breed off them and hopefully produce a strain capable of winning at club level at least. He had got rid of all his old pigeons and was prepared to start from scratch.

But first there was the matter of building a new, improved loft. And he wanted the loft built quickly. If he didn't move soon Des Keogh might give the birds to another fancier. So he took an added interest in what was due to happen to the old house across the fields. There was talk that it was going to be demolished to make way for a new development.

One day a van full of workmen arrived. As soon as the men were out of the van a JCB arrived. Luke ran over and told them he planned to build a pigeon-loft and could they keep him some floor-boards, joists, and a few doors? The men kindly put aside a pile of planks and doors, before taking the raised bucket of the JCB to the walls and shoving the whole structure to the ground to use as dry filling for the new development. Hammer and Gavin helped to carry the planks and doors across the fields to Luke's back yard.

Luckily, his father and his older brother John, offered to build the loft. The floor was raised on concrete blocks, and the roof was slated with slates from the old house. A gap was left in the wall for a trap through which the pigeons could enter. Luke thought of using mesh and bob-bars but his father told him he would give him a sputnik trap.

'A sputnik trap? What's that?' asked Gavin, trying to sound interested.

'It's a landing platform and an entrance for the pigeons to get into the loft. It's very handy.'

'Couldn't you use some wood as a platform just as easily – and have a small opening for the pigeons? It'd probably work out much cheaper.'

'No, a sputnik is far better. It gets the pigeons in quicker after a race.'

'What do you mean?'

'Well, once a pigeon lands and goes into the trap the bars on the trap close and the pigeon can't get back out again. And you can reach into the sputnik from inside the loft and catch the pigeon to clock it without losin' any vital flyin' time. There 's no point in doing a Mickey Mouse job. If you're racin', you must have a sputnik. Otherwise you could spend half the day tryin' to catch a pigeon to clock it.

'And sputniks are handy to let youngsters into before lettin' them out for the first time. It gives them a kind of an idea of what to expect. It makes a real difference.'

'I hope you do well with it.'

'Course I will. All I want is the right pigeons.'

It took Luke's father the best part of his two weeks' holiday to finish the loft, though Hammer and Gavin unselfishly gave a hand. Jake was too busy hidden away somewhere practising on his guitar and experimenting with his song writing.

Once the main structure of the loft was built, there was enough wood left over to fit out the inside. The space was divided into three sections; one for stock birds, another for youngsters and hens to be segregated from time to time, and a third for the birds he intended to race. The rest of the wood was used to build a shelf-like series of perches and nesting-boxes.

When the loft was finally finished, it was all he could

wish for, and more. The trial and error of the last year was, hopefully, over. This time he would be properly prepared and advised.

The racing season was in full swing. But he wouldn't be ready to race until the following season, at least. First he would have to pick up the pigeons from Des Keogh. Then he would have to breed a few youngsters off them, probably the following March. He intended to rear and train the young birds and have them ready to race in the young bird races nearer the end of the April to September season. He didn't intend to race the old birds at all – just breed off them.

Racing entailed the hefty cost of buying a racing-clock (when the pigeons came back from a race they had to be clocked-in on a racing-clock which recorded the exact time of arrival). He nearly had enough money and hoped to buy one at Christmas. Then he could work on raising the club fees by summer.

As soon as the loft was built, he got his father to drive him into Bray to collect the pigeons Des Keogh had promised him – three cocks and three hens.

'They're matched pairs. Though I shoulda thought of it . . . I could have given you a few eggs to hatch out that day I met you at the harbour.'

'Eggs?'

'Yeah. You could have put them under a hen to hatch out. Lotsa pigeon men do that. If they're overbreedin' sometimes they give eggs to fanciers that aren't doin' that well. Birdmen do the same. Got the loft built?'

'It's finished. Want to come out and look at it?'

'Mightn't be a bad idea. I'd be able to give you a few tips to see that you set everythin' up right.'

'Come out on Sunday then.'

'Right, Sunday.'

When Luke got back to Greystones he immediately put the pigeons into his loft. He could hardly wait for the time to come to breed some youngsters off them. But he was to acquire his best youngsters in quite a different way.

The Sunday after Luke finished building the loft Jake resurfaced. The occasion was a solo concert he intended giving outside the Arcade at Greystones harbour. He sneaked into the shop inside the entrance, unplugged the whipped ice-cream machine and plugged the extension leads from his new electric guitar and amplifier into the socket. He went back outside and began the concert. A crowd of local boppers began to gather around. He began to play real hard, real loud. And the more frantically and the longer he played the softer the ice-cream and cones began to get inside the shop. He was building up to a grand finale, thinking what a pity it was he hadn't got a microphone, when all of a sudden the amplifier became as dead as a stuffed duck. The woman from the shop came running out, her fingers dripping in melted ice-cream. She clipped him on the ear and told him to clear off. The crowd began to laugh. But Jake didn't care. He calmly rolled up the extension lead, picked up his guitar and amplifier, and walked off. No, he didn't care in the least. He was too busy in the throes of making a name for himself. The road to fame and fortune was bound to be rocky, if not slippery, but he was determined to stick it out.

Through the idle days of summer, Gavin kept rigorously to his training programme. At times he felt he should go to see Elaine's father to have a chat with him. Should he be canvassing his wares to a Dublin club? If he didn't get an offer by September, that would be another year gone. He always ended up by putting the decision on the long finger; another week could do no harm.

Late in August Shamrock Boys played in a pre-season five-a-side in Booterstown Park just opposite Willow Park School. Most of the participating teams were from prominent schoolboy clubs on the south side. Only they didn't use their official club names for the tournament. The Shamrock Boys became the Red Devils. Three games were listed for each night, with three separate competitions: U-9, U-15 and a senior one for men. The under-age sections were based on the age groups for the coming season.

Gavin's team got to the final. After the semi-final, a man he had noticed on the sidelines during the tournament approached him. He was pretty fit looking (probably played some junior football on the side), well-tanned, wearing a short-sleeved shirt and blue denim jeans. He looked very casual, very easy-going. Instinctively Gavin knew that this was the moment he had been waiting for.

'Any chance of playing for us this season?'

'Under fifteen?'

'Yes.'

'What's the team?'

'Cambridge Boys. The best. We play out of Ringsend.'

'My mother's people are from Ringsend.'

'What's their names?'

'Charlie and Mary Curran.'

'Know them. The live just across the road from Shelbourne Park.'

'That's them. Listen, I'd have to check it out with my parents to see if it would be all right to play and . . . how am I to get to Ringsend?'

'I've a mate lives in Bray. He'll pick you up in Greystones – leave you back after. Only thing, you'll have to get the Dart in Bray. Get off at Sandymount. I'll pick you up there and bring you to the pitch.'

'We're playin' here in the final on Sunday. I'll let you know then if I'm allowed to play or not. Will you be here?'

'You bet I will. What time's kick-off?'

'About eight.'

'Any chance of your mate signing?'

'Who, Hammer?'

'The big fellow at the back.'

'No, he won't sign. I'll ask him though.'

'That girl by the way . . . ?'

Elaine was also on the Red Devils team. Her father had come to all the matches with her.

'What about her?'

'She's a real good one. Would she be interested in playing for a ladies' team down our way?'

'No, she's more into athletics. We just got her for this tournament. Though it would be nice to ask her. The organizers gave the OK. She's more or less given up soccer.'

'Right, Sunday then. I'll bring a League registration form. If you're happy you can sign on the spot. Ask your man, Hammer. I'll bring a form for him too.'

'Don't bother to bring a form for Hammer. You'd only be wastin' your time.'

'I'm doing that all me life. See you Sunday.'

When Gavin got home he told his parents of his prospective move to a Dublin team.

Jimmy Byrne objected. 'You can't leave Shamrock Boys.'

'But I want to. I've got a good chance of a schoolboy cap if I'm playin' in Dublin.'

'Who told you that?'

'Nobody. I just know so. I'd have a better chance of gettin' on if I played in Dublin.'

'Talk about big heads.'

It was his father talking. So far his mother had said nothing. She didn't feel she had to. It was Gavin's decision. It was up to him to decide.

'If you leave Shamrock Boys,' his father said, 'you won't be very popular. Your friends won't like it. The club'll be down here tearin' me door down.'

'They already know I'm leavin'.'

'When did you tell them?'

'I'm sick tellin' them all summer.'

'Think of me. I won't have a minute's peace. They'll be pesterin' me, annoyin' me. They'll have it in for me.'

'There'll be nothing about it. Anything to be said has already been said. I want a chance of a schoolboy cap.'

'And if ye don't get it after all that travellin' into Dublin, don't blame me.'

'If I don't get it, I don't get it. End of story.'

'Who's fillin' yer head with all these notions of a schoolboy cap? Next you'll want to play in England.'

'That's the idea of the schoolboy cap. With a little luck it'll lead to a trial with an English League team.'

'God! This is gettin' strong. England! What club are ye thinkin' of joinin' in Dublin anyway?'

'Cambridge Boys.'

'They're from Ringsend,' said his mother.

'Ringsend . . . ?' His father was softening slightly.

'Yeah. They play in Ringsend Park. It's only down the road from where Granny and Granda live.'

' "Iodine Park", that's what they used to call it.' His mother was thinking back. You could see that faraway look in her eye. The slight smile on her face. She was from Ringsend herself. Her younger brother had played out of Ringsend Park for a team called Bolton Athletic. Top priority for the team's medical kit had been some iodine. The players were always cutting themselves, hence the name 'Iodine Park'.

'There's nothin' wrong with him goin' to Ringsend, Jimmy. Sure it's his second home.'

'Nothin' wrong? What about the travellin'? What about the expense?'

'It's all bein' looked after.'

'Right, son. Have it your way. You know best. But first thing I'm goin' out and buyin' a pair of earplugs. I'm not goin' to put up with everyone barkin' at me over you leavin' Shamrock Boys.'

'There'll be no barkin'. It's all over and done with.'

Gavin's mother looked peeved. 'Jimmy, he could do worse than join a team from Ringsend. Nearly all the great football players come from Ringsend. Where do you think he got it from?'

'What about my side of the family?'

Gavin's mother put her hands on her hips. 'That one I'm still tryin' to figure out. God knows where I got you from.'

Jimmy Byrne smiled. 'He does an' all. You got me in the Arcadia dance-hall in Bray. Remember?'

She remembered.

The final of the U-15 tournament started at 8.15 on Sunday night. The Red Devils were down to play Leicester Celtic who played out of Marley Park. The pitch was miniature sized. The goals were small, something like in hockey. No players, bar the goalkeepers were allowed to play the ball inside the penalty areas. Usual procedure on tactics was two at the back with one pushing into midfield. The other two outfield players had to work in tandem, running the midfield and the attack. Also, a defender was used to take all frees and corners. Five-a-side was a very fast, all-action energy-sapping game, even though the games were only of thirty minutes duration.

The Red Devils had a lad called Simon Nolan in goal. Hammer and Rasher Murphy held the back, with Hammer filtering into midfield. Elaine and Gavin did the grafting in midfield and up front. Robert Smyth and Mousey Burke were the two subs.

There was a large crowd of spectators at the finals. Elaine's father had made it too, and he brought Jake and Luke in the car. It was Luke's first time at a match in ages. And it was the first time he had ever met Elaine. Jake had asked her beforehand if he could bring Luke with him.

The U-9s got under way first. The Wombles, from the Cambridge Boys stable, won.

The U-15 final took place: The Red Devils v The Undertakers. The Undertakers were Leicester Celtic.

The Red Devils played well and the score finished two-all. The match went to extra time. Elaine scored. The Undertakers equalized. Extra time finished all square. The Red Devils won 5-4 on penalties. It was a big feather in Shamrock Boys cap. Most of the top teams from Dublin's southside had taken part in the tournament. The Red Devils were total underdogs. They had come from nowhere and won the competition. But it was hardly surprising when they had players of the calibre of Gavin, Hammer and Elaine.

When the match was over Gavin looked around for the Cambridge U-15 manager. He couldn't see him anywhere. Luckily, the Wombles manager was still at the pitch.

Gavin went over to him.

'Excuse me. Are you involved with Cambridge Boys?'

'So what if I am?'

'I was to meet your U-15 manager here. He hasn't shown up.'

'Probably got delayed in traffic. Had to bring the wife and kids to Brittas Bay. Give him a chance. Wait until the men's match is over. He's keen on you. Hold on a few minutes, he might be here by then.'

Gavin went over to Gerry Horgan.

'Gerry, can you wait awhile? I want to see a man.'

'Not likely. We're goin' now. Get in the van. I ain't waitin' around here for you to sign for another club.'

On the way in from Greystones to the tournament Gerry Horgan had produced a Wicklow League registration form. Gavin had declined to sign it. Whereupon Robert Smyth blurted out that Gavin wasn't signing for Shamrock Boys, that he was going to sign for Cambridge Boys instead.

'Just give's twenty minutes.'

'Not likely. We're goin'. We want nothin' to do with you

signin' for Cambridge Boys.'

'Gerry . . .'

'Forget about it. Either come now, or get the bus home.'

'But, Gerry . . .'

Gerry Horgan didn't want to know. He picked up the kit-bag and walked towards the road, where the van was parked. The players followed him. Hammer just shrugged.

Gavin stayed put. If Elaine's father hadn't been at the match he would have been stranded. He hadn't got the bus fare. He was stony broke. He asked Mr Clarke to hold on until the men's match got under way. Hopefully the Cambridge manager would show up before it was over.

By half-time in the senior final the Cambridge U-15 manager still hadn't arrived. Gavin began to feel anxious. What if the man didn't show up? Now that he had committed himself he'd feel a right fool if the Cambridge manager gave him the cold shoulder. He stood on the sideline beside Elaine, her father, Luke and Jake, not knowing what to think. He felt numb. Everything around him was unreal. He kept a half-eye on the green margin that led to the road; a half-eye on the match. He found it hard to concentrate. Hell, the Cambridge manager had better show up . . . He'd better show up.

The match was only fifteen minutes a side. It was nearly over. Gavin was praying for extra-time. There was no score. There were only seconds left. The red team got a free kick just outside the penalty-area. The referee put his hand in the air and indicated for an indirect free.

'Indirect, ref?' asked a few of the opposing players.

'Certainly. Indirect.'

The free was taken. It passed the wall without touching anyone. The goalkeeper let it go into the net. (Being indirect, it would have had to be played, or touched, by another player before the goal would be allowed.)

The referee blew his whistle and pointed towards the centre-circle.

Pandemonium.

'Ref, nobody touched it.'

'Ref, you signalled an indirect free.'

'Signalled! He *said* it was an indirect free.'

'I said it was direct . . . it's a goal.'

The players began to argue.

Somebody shoved the referee.

Scuffles broke out all over the pitch.

'Someone ring for the Guards.'

The Gardai weren't long in arriving. They were more or less on the Booterstown Road anyway. They escorted the referee from the melee. Told him to grab his clothes. They put him in the back of the squad-car for his own protection and drove him home.

The game hadn't finished. The two teams were left to fight over who won the trophies. When it was all sorted out that was the end of football tournaments in Booterstown Park.

Just as the referee was being escorted to safety by the Gardai someone tapped Gavin on the shoulder.

'Here's the registration form. Sorry I'm late.'

Cambridge Boys U-15 manager had finally got free of the Sunday evening traffic-jams and made it to the pitch.

Gavin signed the form.

As of the next day, when his new manager posted the form to the League registration office, Gavin was a Cambridge Boys player.

7

Gavin didn't get straight into the first eleven. He played in the pre-season friendlies, but for the opening League game he was listed in the subs. He knew that he would have to fight hard to make the first. Cambridge Boys were certainly a top-class outfit. They had gone through the previous season unbeaten, and won every competition that was open to them. And it was tipped that at least five of the squad would make the Irish Schoolboys panel.

Apart from only being a sub at the outset, Gavin was getting some stick, especially from the incumbent centre-forward.

'How's all in the country?'

'How's the cabbage comin' on?'

'Ri', don't play the ball to Dinny. He might bring it back to Glenroe.'

'There's a hen clockin' in yer knicks, country boy.'

The remarks were always made out of earshot of the manager. Gavin didn't quite know how to handle the situation. He felt very despondent and at times was on the verge of chucking it in.

A few Sundays into the season, Cambridge were at home to Lourdes Celtic. Mr Clarke was at the match. He had dropped Elaine off at the Crusaders club for an athletics meet later that afternoon and then driven over to Ringsend Park to get the second half. He could see things weren't going too well for Gavin. When he came on for the last twenty minutes, he didn't seem to be trying. Mr Clarke felt that there was something wrong. Then, just at the end of the match, he heard two of the players jeering Gavin. He decided to have a word with the manager while the teams were getting changed.

'How long has this been going on?'

'What?'

'The players calling Gavin names.'

'Calling him names? That's the first I knew of it.'

'Well, it's happening. I heard it. And it wasn't nice. Has he been playing this badly all along?'

'No. It's only the last few weeks. He's probably going through a patch.'

'He's unhappy. You'll have to sort out whoever's calling him names. I'm not trying to tell you your job. But there's something going on and it's up to you to put an end to it.'

'Mister, I appreciate what you're saying. But it's not easy to watch everything that's going on. What with getting nets up, looking for keys, keeping an eye on equipment. Not to mention the lads! But I'll look into it.'

'I hope you do.'

'You have my word on it.'

When Gavin came out of the pavilion Mr Clarke said nothing about his chat with the Cambridge manager.

'Elaine's running in a club meet down at Crusaders. Would you like to come?'

'Sure.'

They got into the car. Mr Clarke asked casually, 'How do you feel about Cambridge Boys?'

'All right.'

'Sure?'

'Yeah.'

Other than that, the talk was about the athletics meet and how Elaine was getting on.

Need it be asked? She was getting on very well. And when Gavin saw her competing in the 800 metres, just watching her scorching around the track seemed to have a happy feel about it. It was great to see, especially after all the hassle over playing with Shamrock Boys. She won her race. Gavin felt she had made the right decision to quit soccer. She was happier being involved in athletics.

He wished he could say the same about himself and Cambridge Boys.

On the way home in the car Elaine was intent on finding out how he was getting on. But Gavin was evasive, didn't sound enthusiastic. Mr Clarke came to his rescue.

'He's doing just fine, Elaine.'

'Sure?'

'Yeah, I'm doin' well enough. We're winnin' all our matches. Everything's fine. How's it goin' in school?' he added, rather lamely.

'Not bad,' frowned Elaine. It was a silly question; she knew only too well that Gavin wasn't the slightest bit interested in how she was doing at school.

'Hammer and Jake were askin' for you. They haven't seen you around in a while. Jake's lookin' around to get a band going. It's not happening for him though.'

'Pity. Tell him to invite me to his first gig. What's your new manager like?'

'He's okay.'

'And the players?'

'Okay'.

'I must come and see you play soon.'

'Don't bother . . . I mean it would put you out. There's no point in comin' all that distance to see me play.'

'But I'd like to see how you're doing.'

'Elaine, don't bother . . . I'd rather if you didn't come.'

Elaine said no more. She just looked at her father and changed the subject. There was something wrong between Cambridge Boys and Gavin. It was obvious that Gavin wasn't happy with the set-up there. Something was amiss.

The following Sunday Cambridge Boys were away to Cherry Orchard in Ballyfermot. Gavin started the game. At first his heart wasn't in it. But the manager encouraged him from the side-line. And the players were that little bit friendlier, excluding the number 9 Gavin had replaced. He sat on the side-line scowling.

'You going to stop your brooding?' asked the manager.

'Wha?'

'You going to stop your shenanagins?'

'Wha?'

'Messing things up for Gavin Byrne.'

'I'm not messin' things.'

'You have been. Either stop it or get out of the team.'

'Honest. I've been doin' nothin'.'

'You will be doing nothing if you don't stop messing Gavin Byrne about.'

During the second half Gavin improved. He showed some nice touches. The following Tuesday at training he got no hassle. Things got better. In another three weeks he was friendly with all the players, including the big number 9. At last he was a part of the team and his true form began to show. He gave Cambridge Boys that extra bite of steel which was to make them invincible.

Before Easter they were so far ahead of the other teams that they were almost out of sight in the League table. Gavin was selected for the Dublin Schoolboys League team. Things were going really well. From a state of near misery, he felt on top of the world.

While Gavin and Cambridge Boys were on the up and up, the U-15 season wasn't going so well for Shamrock Boys.

All the old teams entered the League with the exception of Ashford and Rathdrum. But Shamrock Boys weren't to figure in the shake-up for League honours. Morale was low after Gavin left. Robert Smyth gave up playing for a while as a result of Gavin leaving.

'Once one leaves, then someone else will leave. The team'll break up.'

'What d'ya mean?'

'Gavin's gone. Hammer will go too, and that will be the end of us. The whole team will just break up.'

'But Hammer ain't leavin'.'

'He will. Once he sees how well Gavin's doing he'll leave. And who could blame him. He never got anywhere playing with us. We're in the outer regions of space here. Hello! is there anyone out there?'

But Robert Smyth was wrong. Hammer didn't leave. And it was not that he didn't get the chance.

One night a man came to his house and asked him if he would play for St Joseph's in Sallynoggin. But Hammer didn't want to. He didn't want to leave Shamrock Boys not unless they broke up. He felt he had a duty to stay. Anyway he didn't really want to go to Sallynoggin. It was too far. The man said he would pick him up every Sunday.

'But what about trainin'?'

'You'll have to make your own way down.'

No. Hammer decided he didn't want to go. Maybe when he turned U-18. Maybe he'd give it a go for his last year in under-age football.

The man left in disappointment, but said he would hold Hammer to his word. He would be back at U-18 level.

'Why go to the bother?' asked Hammer.

The man laughed. 'Because now you're a dark horse, but some day you're goin' to be a winner.'

Hammer never forgot those words.

Soon afterwards, when Robert Smyth heard that Hammer had turned down St Joseph's he came back to Shamrock Boys. They began to play with more enthusiasm, and took a keener interest in training. The knowledge that Hammer wasn't up for grabs gave them fresh heart. Hammer was the heart of Shamrock Boys. Lose Hammer and the team would die. All the players knew that. Even Gummy Davis.

As a result of the new-found enthusiasm Gerry Horgan said he would do his best to organize a trip to North Wales for Easter. That really pepped the lads and inspired them to put in a good run for the Cup, whatever about the opportunities that had gone abegging in the League.

The trip to North Wales was a real lark. The fun started on the ship. The whole squad went, including Jake. They had all put a few bob into the kitty towards the trip. That is, all except Jake. He invited himself along.

'I'm just goin' as far as the boat with yous.'

When they got to the terminal in Dun Laoghaire Jake went in with them. He got to the gangway without being checked.

'You better go home now.'

'I don't know. If I got this far I might get on the ship without being spotted.'

'But you've no ticket. Somewhere along the line you're goin' to be asked to show a ticket.'

'That's where you're wrong. It's a group ticket. They're not goin' to hold up everybody to try and count us.'

'But Gerry Horgan won't like it.'

'I'll hide from him until we get to the far side. Then it'll be too late for him to do anything about it.'

'He'll go ape.'

'Doesn't matter. I won't get caught.'

The first Gerry Horgan knew of Jake's presence was on the train from Holyhead to Llandudno Junction. He spotted him in the middle of a card-game with some of the lads. There wasn't much he could do about it at that stage. Jake gave him a smile and a wink for his troubles.

'Where are you going to sleep?'

'On the floor of wherever you're stayin'.'

'I hope you brought spending money.'

'Spendin' money? Who needs spendin' money? Sure isn't this the Welfare State?'

Their destination, Llandudno, was a pretty place, pretty and old-fashioned. Pretty and by the sea. As they were staying in self-catering flats, it was easy for Jake to blend in. There was no head count. It was just a simple matter of rooms, no supervision, though the manager did have an office downstairs. You could have brought in a non-paying army and hidden them, much less Jake.

They had a marvellous weekend. Unknown to Gerry Horgan some of the lads helped themselves to a few free 'souvenirs' from the shops, and had enough presents packed in their bags to give the Customs a busy hour or two on their return to Dun Laoghaire.

On the Saturday night Jake went missing. He couldn't be found anywhere. At eleven-thirty they called the search off. Gerry Horgan wasn't too worried. He and two of the adults who had come along on the trip went to a nightclub along the Promenade to unwind. They got some surprise when they saw Jake onstage giving the band a helping hand. He was playing the guitar.

By the time they left the flats the manager had had enough of them, 'Six broken bedsprings. Three torn sheets. A rip in a settee. Please, don't come back.' He was glad to see the end of them. But Shamrock Boys had happy memories of Llandudno, whatever memories Llandudno had of them.

Their last abiding memory of the trip was getting off the train in Holyhead. A drunken republican, draped around a lamp-post, was shouting, 'Burn the train. It's included in the fare.'

Hammer took a poor view of the events of the weekend. Lar Holmes would have kept a stricter eye on things he felt. He was disappointed in Shamrock Boys.

The trip to North Wales proved a real tonic for Shamrock Boys. They reached the final of the Wicklow Cup. The opposition was their lovable adversaries – Riverside Boys. Harry Hennessy was down to ref.

'Look at his belly. Bigger than ever.'

'At least ten inches bigger.'

'He'll burst.'

'Know what he reminds me of?'

'No. What?'

'A giant Easter egg on wheels.'

Shamrock Boys had a new strip for the final. It was green with a white zag going across the chest. They didn't think much of their chances but they were all geared up to give it their best shot. Gerry Horgan had decided on a new formation: 5-3-2. The players couldn't fully understand how it operated. Not even Hammer.

'You see, you play a sweeper behind the defence.'

Jaws dropped open. 'A wha?' 'A sweeper?'

'Yip. Apart from defence, a sweeper means anyone can break from the back, be it the fulls or the central defenders. You see, the sweeper can cover the player that breaks. It means you can bring in defenders as attackers and still not leave yourself open at the back. Understand?'

'No.'

Neither did Riverside Boys. They were all out to give Shamrock Boys a traditional Riverside stuffing. But this strange-fangled idea of using a sweeper to set up attacks had them bamboozled. They found themselves being pushed back into their own half of the field all the time. Even Harry Hennessy was having trouble giving them frees in favourable positions. It was odds on Shamrock Boys were going to cause an upset. But the inevitable happened, Riverside cracked the sweeper system for once and scored a well-worked goal. There was no comeback for Shamrock Boys. They were beaten. They had lost a cup final for the second year on the trot.

Riverside, for their part, did a lap of honour, and didn't bother to get changed. They got straight into Mr. Glynn's battered Opel estate and headed back down Dargle side.

Somewhere along the way they met Chopper Doyle.

'D'ya wanna lift?'

'Naw. Not interested in cars any more. Goin' to be a jockey.'

Gavin progressed very quickly under the tutelage of Cambridge Boys. Just a few months short of his sixteenth birthday the rumour went round that he might be picked for the Irish Schoolboys team. There had been a few trial matches and word was leaked to the Cambridge manager that Gavin was very much in the picture. Still, even with the advance speculation, Gavin was on a total high when official word came through that he had made the team. Picked to represent his country! He felt it was the biggest thing that had ever happened to him. Elaine, her father, Hammer, Luke and Jake were all delighted for him. And his family was so proud of him, even his sister, who claimed to be the non-soccer enthusiast of all time. His little brother was totally over the moon. His brother an international footballer! Going to play for Ireland! There was even a buzz at school. And Shamrock Boys weren't slow to tell the local paper that Gavin was a product of their schoolboy system, even if nowadays he was a registered Cambridge Boys player. Every time he walked through Greystones heads would turn and offer congratulations. He felt great. Those were heady days.

His first international cap was against Denmark, his second against Germany. Both were occasions to remember.

The match against Denmark was played in Cork. All the selected Dublin players met at Heuston Station. The Dublin-based SFAI officials were also there, resplendent in the national association's crested blazers.

'See Joey, there.'

'Wonder if he's comin' on the train or jus' seein' us off!'

Joey was a top Dublin Schoolboys official and on the executive of the SFAI. He was a nice old gentleman, a favourite of the players. But they always took advantage of his good nature by cadging off him.

'Hey, Joey, I'm thirsty. What about a can of coke?'

'Joey, I'm hungry. What about a Mars bar?'

'Hey, Joey. I could do with a smoke. Give's one.'

'You're not supposed to smoke.'

'Oh, I forgot. How about a few drags, then?'

Joey, a real gentleman, *was* going with them. The players perked up. They knew they were in for a good weekend.

They sat quietly on the train playing cards and chatting, discussing the tactics and formation they knew the manager would use. They were well drilled, well prepared. The squad sessions had been going on for the previous two months. As far as the Dublin Schoolboys were concerned, they had more get-togethers than some club teams. The squad was always brought together at U-13 level and the elite then graduated to the Irish Schoolboys panel. It was the same with a lot of the country leagues. They brought their best players together at an early age, and the screening process was quite intense.

One interesting topic came up on the train.

'Hear there's some English kid bein' brought into the squad in a few weeks.'

'English kid?'

'Yeah, English. His parents are Irish.'

'I thought they didn't bring them in until Youth level.'

'Yeah, that's right. But this kid's caused a real stir. He was selected for the English School of Excellence course run by the FA. Showed up wearin' an Irish strip. They all looked goggle-eyed at him. Took him off the course when he said his ambition was to play for Ireland. He'll be in our squad later on. Joey told me all about it.'

'That's good. A real good one.'

'Yeah, isn't it? Takes some beatin'. Only when he gets into the squad one of us will have to get off.'

The Danish match was played the next day at Turner's Cross. Gavin felt nervous before the game. All the build-up, the staying overnight in a hotel, the pre-match training session, the over-seriousness of the talks, was unsettling him. He was glad to get out on the pitch. Glad to get the match over with.

suppose I got the chance to go to England?'

n't know. Would you want to go?'

...'

t about your Junior Cert?'

hat?'

r father would have to agree. Anyway, never mind
d. What are you going to do now?'

own to the Railway Field.'

go to the Railway Field?'

ads will be there.'

should be at school.'

w. But they'll want to know how I got on after the

don't forget to ring Mr Mooney.'

n't. There's a phone-box near the Railway Field.'

ished his breakfast and put the papers to one side,
them open at the sports page. He knew his mother
want to cut out the match reports and add them to
e-ups of the game played against Denmark. One
g from that game described him as 'a teenage
n'.

d good-bye to his mother and hurried through the
estate, taking a short-cut to the Railway Field.

er, Luke and Jake were waiting, sitting on top of
ay embankment. Jake was playing a guitar. (It was
heap type he used for messing around with; the
Coy, an electric Yamaha plus amplifier, was at
The other two sat dozily listening to the smooth
The tune was something instrumental, something
ast age of rock music, something once played by a
lled The Shadows. When they saw Gavin come
ield, Jake broke off his playing.

wheeled by on the top ridge of the embankment.
nd shook.

ree lads had plenty of questions about the game
swered for a while, then cut them short. 'There

In the dressing-room before the match he was handed a
telex. It was a good luck message from Elaine and her
father. Gavin appreciated the gesture. Only the weekend
before, he had heard that she had won the Leinster Schools
Intermediate 800 metres title. And that she was shortly due
to run in the All-Ireland Schools Championships. He
hadn't seen much of her lately but he followed her
progress through the papers.

They played a 4-3-3 system against Denmark. Gavin
played up front. The Danes were good. Excellent on the
ball and very quick. International football was fast. The
game could slow down at times, but then it could spurt.
Some players couldn't adapt to the pace. But technique
was also important. Pace and technique were the twin
rocks on which some players' international prospects
foundered. They could be very good at club level, but
playing at the highest grade – that was the true test of a
player's ability, and the higher the standard, the greater the
casualties.

The atmosphere wasn't great. But that didn't really
matter to the players. It was the thrill of wearing the green
of Ireland, of representing their country for the very first
time that mattered. Even though there were only a few
hundred people present, mostly schoolchildren, it left a
lump in the players' throats. They felt very emotional,
proud to have progressed this far, especially when
thousands of other kids never stood a chance of being
picked to represent their country.

At a throw-in near the corner flag Gavin moved for the
ball. Just as he played it he heard a voice call from the green
clay-banked terracing. 'Come on, Gavin!' It was a woman's
voice. Gavin turned around and saw his mother and father
standing beside the low boundary wall beyond the side-
line. They gave him a wave. He hadn't expected them to be
at the match. They had said nothing, travelling south at the
last minute. They didn't want to miss seeing their son

playing for Ireland. They were as proud as Punch, especially his mother with her strong Ringsend tradition.

The play was fifty-fifty. But basically it was a learning process for both teams – their first taste of international football. Next time out, both would be less nervous, much more mature. The game was one of contrasting styles. Ireland with their bustling never-say-die attitude, and the Danes with their fluid Continental football.

'Dessie! Dessie!' the local supporters were cheering their own home-bred hero every time he touched the ball. 'Dessie . . . ! Des - sie . . . ! Go Dessie . . . ! Go Dessie! Go!'

Dessie duly obliged. He scored both of Ireland's goals in a narrow 2-1 win. The crowd was pleased. In a team dominated by Dubliners, one of their own had set up the victory. Nobody could tell them that the goals were made by Gavin – all Dessie had to do was to tap the ball into the net.

As for Gavin, he had adapted well to schoolboy international football. He was nominated Man of the Match.

After the game, on the train journey back to Dublin, one of the players took an Irish number 11 jersey from his bag.

'Hey, you're supposed to give that back.'

'I know. I nicked it.'

'Playin' for Ireland and you nicked the jersey. You ought to be ashamed.'

'I nicked this too.' He took an Irish goalkeeper's jersey from his bag.

'Did you take any more?'

'No, I couldn't fit them all into one bag.'

'Just as well. They'd have to call our next match off. There'd have been no gear left to play in. What are you goin' to do with the gear anyway?'

'Me manager had a meetin' last week. Asked us to think of ways to make money for the club. Well, the jerseys are my contribution. I'm goin' to raffle them.'

'We're playin' Germany in a few weeks. Don't take any

more jerseys then or there won't be a [Got me?'

'Gotcha.'

The morning after Gavin's second sc[Germany, he slept late. He had bee[school. He got out of bed at about [sweat-shirt inside his jeans and gave[the chipped Doc Marten boots shove[the wardrobe. He bent down to pick t[his mind. Instead he put on a pair of [bedroom window the sun slanted [council houses. He went downstairs[his mother handed him the morn[thanked her, sat beside the table an[sports pages. The house was quiet [younger brother and sister were at sc[

'Young Stars Outgun Germans,' re['Ireland Dumps Germans,' read an[He checked to see if his own na[any of the reports. 'Ma, I'm in them [

But his mother already knew. She [corner shop at seven-thirty, bough[before she had time to look the sh[about the reports.

'What do you want for breakfast, ['Whatever is handiest.'

'Gavin, don't forget to ring Mr M['I won't, Ma.'

Mr Mooney was the manager [team. It seemed that English Leagu[the game and afterwards Mr M[were rumours that the scouts were[me tomorrow, between half-eleve[have more news by then.' Gavin [heart set on playing professional f[

In the dressing-room before the match he was handed a telex. It was a good luck message from Elaine and her father. Gavin appreciated the gesture. Only the weekend before, he had heard that she had won the Leinster Schools Intermediate 800 metres title. And that she was shortly due to run in the All-Ireland Schools Championships. He hadn't seen much of her lately but he followed her progress through the papers.

They played a 4-3-3 system against Denmark. Gavin played up front. The Danes were good. Excellent on the ball and very quick. International football was fast. The game could slow down at times, but then it could spurt. Some players couldn't adapt to the pace. But technique was also important. Pace and technique were the twin rocks on which some players' international prospects foundered. They could be very good at club level, but playing at the highest grade – that was the true test of a player's ability, and the higher the standard, the greater the casualties.

The atmosphere wasn't great. But that didn't really matter to the players. It was the thrill of wearing the green of Ireland, of representing their country for the very first time that mattered. Even though there were only a few hundred people present, mostly schoolchildren, it left a lump in the players' throats. They felt very emotional, proud to have progressed this far, especially when thousands of other kids never stood a chance of being picked to represent their country.

At a throw-in near the corner flag Gavin moved for the ball. Just as he played it he heard a voice call from the green clay-banked terracing. 'Come on, Gavin!' It was a woman's voice. Gavin turned around and saw his mother and father standing beside the low boundary wall beyond the side-line. They gave him a wave. He hadn't expected them to be at the match. They had said nothing, travelling south at the last minute. They didn't want to miss seeing their son playing for Ireland. They were as proud as Punch, especially his mother with her strong Ringsend tradition.

The play was fifty-fifty. But basically it was a learning process for both teams – their first taste of international football. Next time out, both would be less nervous, much more mature. The game was one of contrasting styles. Ireland with their bustling never-say-die attitude, and the Danes with their fluid Continental football.

'Dessie! Dessie!' the local supporters were cheering their own home-bred hero every time he touched the ball. 'Dessie . . . ! Des - sie . . . ! Go Dessie . . . ! Go Dessie! Go!'

Dessie duly obliged. He scored both of Ireland's goals in a narrow 2-1 win. The crowd was pleased. In a team dominated by Dubliners, one of their own had set up the victory. Nobody could tell them that the goals were made by Gavin – all Dessie had to do was to tap the ball into the net.

As for Gavin, he had adapted well to schoolboy international football. He was nominated Man of the Match.

After the game, on the train journey back to Dublin, one of the players took an Irish number 11 jersey from his bag.

'Hey, you're supposed to give that back.'

'I know. I nicked it.'

'Playin' for Ireland and you nicked the jersey. You ought to be ashamed.'

'I nicked this too.' He took an Irish goalkeeper's jersey from his bag.

'Did you take any more?'

'No, I couldn't fit them all into one bag.'

'Just as well. They'd have to call our next match off. There'd have been no gear left to play in. What are you goin' to do with the gear anyway?'

'Me manager had a meetin' last week. Asked us to think of ways to make money for the club. Well, the jerseys are my contribution. I'm goin' to raffle them.'

'We're playin' Germany in a few weeks. Don't take any

more jerseys then or there won't be a Dub left on the team. Got me?'

'Gotcha.'

The morning after Gavin's second schoolboy cap, against Germany, he slept late. He had been given the day off school. He got out of bed at about half-ten, tucked his sweat-shirt inside his jeans and gave a hesitant glance at the chipped Doc Marten boots shoved beneath the rim of the wardrobe. He bent down to pick them up, but changed his mind. Instead he put on a pair of sneakers. Outside the bedroom window the sun slanted over the grey-slated council houses. He went downstairs to the kitchen where his mother handed him the morning newspapers. He thanked her, sat beside the table and flicked through the sports pages. The house was quiet – mainly because his younger brother and sister were at school.

'Young Stars Outgun Germans,' read one report.

'Ireland Dumps Germans,' read another.

He checked to see if his own name was mentioned in any of the reports. 'Ma, I'm in them all!'

But his mother already knew. She had been down to the corner shop at seven-thirty, bought the papers, and even before she had time to look the shopkeeper had told her about the reports.

'What do you want for breakfast, Gavin?'

'Whatever is handiest.'

'Gavin, don't forget to ring Mr Mooney.'

'I won't, Ma.'

Mr Mooney was the manager of the Irish Schoolboys team. It seemed that English League scouts were present at the game and afterwards Mr Mooney told Gavin there were rumours that the scouts were interested in him. 'Ring me tomorrow, between half-eleven and twelve. I should have more news by then.' Gavin felt excited. He had his heart set on playing professional football in England.

'Ma, suppose I got the chance to go to England?'

'I don't know. Would you want to go?'

'Yeah.'

'What about your Junior Cert?'

'So what?'

'Your father would have to agree. Anyway, never mind England. What are you going to do now?'

'Go down to the Railway Field.'

'Why go to the Railway Field?'

'The lads will be there.'

'They should be at school.'

'I know. But they'll want to know how I got on after the match.'

'Well, don't forget to ring Mr Mooney.'

'I won't. There's a phone-box near the Railway Field.'

He finished his breakfast and put the papers to one side, leaving them open at the sports page. He knew his mother would want to cut out the match reports and add them to the write-ups of the game played against Denmark. One heading from that game described him as 'a teenage sensation'.

He said good-bye to his mother and hurried through the housing estate, taking a short-cut to the Railway Field.

Hammer, Luke and Jake were waiting, sitting on top of the railway embankment. Jake was playing a guitar. (It was only a cheap type he used for messing around with; the real McCoy, an electric Yamaha plus amplifier, was at home.) The other two sat dozily listening to the smooth chords. The tune was something instrumental, something from a past age of rock music, something once played by a group called The Shadows. When they saw Gavin come into the field, Jake broke off his playing.

A train wheeled by on the top ridge of the embankment. The ground shook.

The three lads had plenty of questions about the game. Gavin answered for a while, then cut them short. 'There were scouts at the match. I've got to ring Mr. Mooney in a few minutes to see if the scouts are interested in me.'

'Imagine if one of the clubs was Liverpool. I'd give me right arm to play for the Pool.'

'Yeah, it'd be great.'

'What about London Albion?'

'Why not? Go to the top!'

'It could be Burnley. They're crap!'

'They weren't always crap,' corrected Hammer. 'Years ago they produced the best young players in England.'

'Crap!'

'It's true!'

The boys fell silent, envious of Gavin. But Hammer's reference to Burnley was true. Once they were on the verge of becoming great but their world had fallen apart.

Jake started to ask Gavin another question but Gavin interrupted him. 'It's time to go to the phone-box.'

'Wha?'

'It's time to ring Mr Mooney.'

The four of them left the Railway Field, Jake with his guitar slung over his shoulder, and headed up the main road to the phone-box.

'Liverpool or United?' mused Hammer.

'Or, Bray Wanderers?' suggested Luke.

But Gavin wasn't listening. He went into the phone-box and Hammer and Luke bundled in after him.

'Who's the lucky club?' asked Jake when they came back.

'He didn't say. Just said to be at Belfield on Tuesday for training, and then I'm off to an international tournament in France in a few weeks. The scouts will be in France. If I'm good enough I'll find out then who's interested in me.'

'Hope it's Liverpool,' said Jake.

'Hope it's London Albion,' said Gavin, and the four of them walked down the hill to the Railway Field.

The sun was hot, but not as hot as it would be in another

month, when the tarmac surface would be sticky and bubbly They sat down near the top of the embankment. Luke took out a deck of cards. They played a few hands, talked of football, talked of France – played a few more hands. Gavin was doing most of the winning.

Some fellows had all the luck.

In between dealing cards they talked a bit. Jake ribbed Hammer.

'You should have joined Cambridge with Gavin.'

'So what?'

'You should have gone with him. You're good enough to do just as well as he did.'

'If I was good enough the selectors' would have taken me from here.'

'They'd never take a player from here. You didn't even get a trial. You should have gone with Gavin and given it a go. You just don't want to bother. That's not me. Some day I'm going to get out of here. I'm going to get a band together. One that plays my kind of music. You won't be seein' me around here much longer.'

'Want to bet?'

'Talkin' of seeing people around,' interrupted Gavin. 'Has anyone seen Elaine lately?'

'She was at the match last night. At the back of the stand with her Ma and Da. At least there's a bit of go in her. She wouldn't spend her time dossin' around Greystones waitin' for the scouts to come and look at her. She'd get out there and put herself in the shop window. That kid's got initiative.'

'Meanin' I haven't?' Hammer was annoyed. 'Ever hear of club loyalty. Well, that's what I've got. *I'm* loyal to my club.'

'Well,' harped Jake, 'where's it gettin' you? Ten years time you'll still be dossin' around Greystones. That's all club loyalty is ever goin' to do for you. Things don't just happen. You've got to get out there and sell yourself.'

'Like you did at Llandudno? That's some advice – comin' from you.'

'I think Jake is right,' said Gavin slowly. 'Remember the old man in the park. He told you.'

'He didn't tell me that.'

'He told you you had ability, didn't he? And Mr Clarke told you what to do with it.'

'That's different. Listen, I'm sick of all this.' He looked at Jake, not at Gavin. 'Do you want to play cards or not? If not go and buzz off. Play with your guitar or somethin'.'

'You want a dig?' retorted Jake.

'Don't make me laugh.'

'Hey, that's enough of that,' restrained Luke. 'Give over.'

'Who asked *you* to butt in?' Jake was really hot under the collar. 'Why don't you go back to your monastery of a pigeon-loft? The only time you come out is when the pigeons are asleep.'

'Easy on,' said Gavin. 'Don't let's spoil everything. Not today. Whose turn is it to deal anyway?'

'Just remember,' fumed Jake, 'some day I'm gettin' out of here and formin' me own band.'

'The sooner the better,' muttered Luke and Hammer together.

'I don't like that remark.'

'Good.'

'Deal a hand and belt up, the three of you.'

'Well, Hammer had better not end up with four aces.'

'And apologize to one another.'

'We apologize.'

Luke dealt a hand.

They quietened. Peace had returned.

Like before, Gavin was still having all the luck.

8

The following Tuesday Gavin took the 84 bus to Belfield for training. He got off at the junction of Foster Avenue and made his way into the Belfield campus through a gate a short way up the Avenue. He followed the path to the walled enclosure where the training session was to be held and went into the pavilion in the corner of the enclosure. Most of the squad were already there. He said 'Hello', and took out his football gear. There was a table in the centre of the room with an assortment of training-bibs thrown in a heap. He picked up one and got changed. The whole set-up was a lot different to the Railway Field in Greystones. It was all very professional, all very serious. There was no messing or fooling around. Everybody was deadly serious.

When they got outside, the training area was segmented into zones marked by plastic cones. The session started with a few warm-up exercises. Then a few laps. Then they divided into groups and played two-touch football, five minutes a side, three a side; they rotated from one marked zone to the next, with one side in turn taking a rest. There then followed a tactical talk. And after that some sprinting and circuit training.

The manager, Mr Mooney, was present, also a coach, a trainer, a sort of all-purpose physio, and two officials who stood watching in the background.

Two players hadn't made it for training, to Mr Mooney's annoyance. One had phoned in to say he had missed his rail connection. The other, who had only newly been called into the squad and had not played in any of the previous matches, had not got in touch. Half way through the session he could be seen coming across the pitch. He had his father with him. He wasn't dressed for training.

The player and his father stood at the side of the training area. They looked worried. Mr Mooney went over to see them. There was a hushed discussion. Then the father and son walked away. The boy seemed to be upset.

'What's wrong, Boss?'

'Shut up!'

'What's wrong?'

'Wait until they're gone.'

Mr Mooney was upset too. He told the trainer to keep the session going, ran after the pair and stood talking to them for a while. He shook the boy's hand and came back. He stopped the training session and told the squad what was wrong.

The boy was over-age, and that was what his father had been explaining. Somewhere along the line the boy's club manager had played him as an over-age player. The practice had continued and only now had the truth come out into the open. It had been left to the father to explain the whole sorry mess.

The training started again. When it was all over Mr Mooney called them into a group.

'This tournament is in France . . . You all know who's in the group . . . Only two go through to the semi-final. Now, there's no need to say thanks for the holiday, 'cause there's goin' to be no holiday. An' there'll be no larkin' about . . . You're representin' your country. Behave yourselves.

'You'll need passports. Get them, an' get them quick. Make a list of what you need to bring. Make sure everything's packed and not left behind. The FAI will supply customary slacks and blazers.

'An' remember, only two teams qualify from the group. We want to be one of those teams. Got it?'

The players nodded in agreement and went back to the dressing-rooms to have a shower and get changed. The subject of the over-age player came up.

'Pity about your man. He's a good player. I played against him last year in one of the national cups. Great comin' forward. Real flier. He must have been playin' over-age all along, maybe since he was eleven or twelve. Whoever his manager was he got him into a right mess.'

'Wha' d'ye mean?'

'It cost him a schoolboy cap, didn't it. That's mess enough. It could ruin him.'

'He didn't have to play over-age. It was his own choice.'

'Maybe not. Maybe there was no team for him at the right age. Maybe the manager was greedy. Who knows? But when you're eleven or twelve all you want is a game. If you can't get a game one way you'll probably take your chance. Maybe it was his only way of gettin' a game.'

'It's still cheatin'. He should have known better.'

'After the first time it probably snowballed on him. Then he couldn't get out.'

'His manager should get done for it.'

'That he should.'

'It turned into a right nightmare. Some people really put their heads on the block . . . Anyone got some soap?'

Half-an-hour later Gavin was standing on the main road outside Belfield, waiting for the bus back to Greystones. Already he was all keyed-up for the trip to France.

By coincidence, a few days later, the All-Ireland Schools track and field events were held at Belfield, only a few hundred yards from where Gavin had trained with the Irish Schoolboys squad. Elaine was down to run the Intermediate 800 metres final at approximately 4.30. She had won the Leinster Intermediate Championships comfortably, and was not expecting any danger from that quarter. Her biggest threat was a girl from Donegal and another from Limerick. The field was fairly tight on the first lap, with no one eager to take up the pace. But on the second lap the girl from Donegal took the lead. Elaine still

100

kept to the middle of the bunch. But when the gap grew a little too wide for comfort she and the Limerick girl quickly reduced the deficit. They surged into the lead on the last three hundred yards. The girl from Donegal resisted. But she wasn't able to hold them off. They left her in their wake. With a hundred yards to go the girl from Limerick broke and Elaine had the tape at her mercy. She had won her first All-Ireland Schools title.

Gavin made the trip to France with the Irish Schoolboys squad. The tournament was played in the Bordeaux area. San Marino, Spain and Belgium were in Ireland's group. France, the host nation, Switzerland, Sweden and Holland were in the other group.

Before they left Ireland they were told they would be staying in a university type campus along with the other teams in their group. The tournament was expensive to stage, possibly it would be badly supported by the general public, so there would have to be cut-backs. Accommodation was an obvious way to save. There wasn't to be the luxury of a hotel for any of the teams.

'Stayin' in a school.'

'It'll be like a concentration camp.'

But the campus wasn't that bad. There was a swimming pool, an indoor sports complex, a running track and at least six soccer pitches.

The Irish squad had flown in from Dublin via Paris, with a connecting flight to Bordeaux. The squad showed only one change from the panel for the home internationals against Denmark and Germany. The kid who had shown up for the English School of Excellence wearing a Republic of Ireland football kit had been added, to the exclusion of the Dubliner who had taken the two football jerseys after the Danish game. His days of taking were over, as were his appearances at schoolboy level for Ireland. The whole squad had learned a lesson. Under no circumstances would there be any messing from here on in. The one rotten apple had been removed from the barrel. From then on, all the lads would be on their best behaviour.

Ireland's first match was against Belgium. Ireland scored first. The ball was played to Gavin off an indirect free kick just outside the Belgian penalty area. The defence was slack. He saw a gap and slammed the ball goalwards. The goalkeeper hadn't a chance. The goal boosted Irish confidence and they laid siege to the Belgian goal. The Irish centre-half headed on the ball from a corner to the near post. Gavin darted in, twisted in a half-leap and headed the ball down on to the goal-line. The Belgian left-full blocked the ball and cleared it off the line up into the stand. He then feigned an injury. But the referee ignored the ploy and allowed play to continue. The left-full made a miraculous recovery, getting up off the ground and running out with his defence to play the off-side trap once the throw-in was taken and played by an Irish boot.

Ireland went close to scoring on several occasions, Belgium on a few. But in the second half the Belgians grew stronger and for the last fifteen minutes the Irish defence was lucky to hold out, that is until, with three minutes to go, Belgium equalized from a header off a free kick.

The game finished. One-all.

The next day was a free day for all the teams in the group and the Irish boys met up with some of the other teams. There was hardly any point. The Irish didn't know Walloon from double Dutch, and the little English the Continentals knew was totally useless when they got talking to one of the Cork players. They couldn't make the slightest headway with his accent.

'Wha . . . t's that . . . ? Indian?'

'No. Cork.'

'Wha . . . t's Cork?'

'It's a country in Ireland.'

'Nor . . . th . . . ern Ireland?'

'No.'

'I thought there were only . . . two countries in Ireland?'

'No, there's four. Dublin, Cork, Culchies and Northern Ireland.'

'Ireland must be big . . . then?'

'Yeah, almost as big as America.'

Ireland's second game was against the group favourites, Spain. They had already trounced San Marino 7-nil. Ireland needed a result. And not just a draw. They needed a win.

The Spanish players were mostly registered with the top Spanish clubs: Real Madrid, Athletico, Barcelona, Seville. They were a very gifted side. But Mr Mooney thought he had a system worked out to counteract their superior skills.

His ploy was thrown into disarray when Gavin got injured after twenty minutes and had to be taken off. It wasn't a serious injury, just a sprained ankle, but it was enough to keep him out for the rest of the tournament.

'Can you put weight on it?'

'Just about.'

'We'll have it X-rayed. Get a stretcher.'

'I don't need one. I can walk.'

'Use the stretcher. It's only a precaution.'

'Look, I can walk.'

Gavin limped off the pitch supported by the coach and the physio.

Half-time, no score. Seventy-six minutes, a goal. Spain one, Ireland nil.

In a stadium on the southern side of Bordeaux, Belgium beat San Marino 5-nil.

To have any chance of qualifying for the semi-finals Ireland needed a big win against San Marino. Something in line with a 7-nil win.

Ireland could have done with Gavin's goal-scoring

prowess against San Marino, but his ankle injury prevented him from playing. They won 5-nil. Later that night when they heard the result of the Spain v Belgium match their worst fears were realized. The game finished in a two-all draw. Ireland was out. The team felt down in the mouth. They had at least hoped for a semi-final place.

The squad was due to fly home the next day. But the fact that they didn't qualify for the semi-finals didn't mean that the tournament was a non-event for Gavin. From his personal viewpoint the excitement only started after Ireland was knocked out at group level. Early the next day, a few hours before the team was due to depart for the airport, Gavin and Mr Mooney were whisked by taxi to one of the top hotels in Bordeaux.

It was enormous. The foyer was full of activity; people checking out, others checking in; porters and bellboys full of French efficiency; mahogany panelling, marble columns and antique furniture resplendent against the high curves of the ornate ceiling.

'What are we doin' here, Mr Mooney?'

'Like I told you in the taxi, it's somethin' special.'

'Like what?'

'Like it's goin' to be one of the most important days in your life.'

They walked up to reception.

'The Garonne Lounge, please.'

Luckily the receptionist spoke English. 'Straight ahead. Second left and first right. Are you meeting someone?'

'Yes, you could say that. We've to meet a few gentlemen. All separately, of course.'

'Is your name Mr Mooney?'

'Yes.'

'Well, a Mr James Norman of Aston Villa is already in the lounge waiting for you.'

They turned from the reception desk and walked across the crowded foyer in the direction of the Garonne Lounge.

'Aston Villa! Why didn't you tell me?'

'Gavin, Aston Villa aren't goin' to be the only ones. There are four others.'

'Who?'

'Manchester United.'

'Who else?'

'Spurs and Arsenal.'

'And . . . ?'

'London Albion.'

All of a sudden Gavin felt excited. The unexpectedness of what Mr Mooney had said took him totally by surprise. He felt light-headed. 'Who are these men? Scouts?'

'Yeah, scouts. But not ordinary scouts. They're the head men.'

The noise and bustle were all around him, but Gavin didn't notice. As soon as he walked into the Garonne Lounge he would come face to face with the representatives of some of the top clubs in the English League. Suddenly, he felt weak. He had never seen a scout until now. But although he had been unaware of their presence they had been watching all season. Like invisible men they had come unannounced, unnoticed; in a park, beside a railing, behind a goal, standing back near the roadway or at the side of a park pavilion. They had been there, mostly at away matches and representative games. Before they had gone home they had taken notes, found out whether he was a devoted footballer, what was his attitude to the game, did he train well, where he lived, whether he was well-behaved or rowdy, if he had ever been in trouble. They had checked on a lot of things, all unknown to him, his manager or his parents.

Now in this Bordeaux hotel, they were about to come out into the open. Initially, they had made their approaches through Mr Mooney. Now they wanted to speak to Gavin. They were interested in a few others in the squad too – some had already been over to England on trials during the Christmas and Easter holidays – but Gavin was their top priority.

This was Gavin's first contact with the cross-channel scene. He had never been anywhere, not until the start of the current season. He had never really played outside Wicklow until a few months ago. Now, the flame that had been kindled at the Railway Field had led to this, sitting down in a hotel in a foreign land talking to the cross-channel scouts, the almost mythical, elusive men, who were often whispered about in dressing-rooms before a match, or after training. At last they had finally surfaced and it was Gavin's turn to experience the sweet taste of their attention.

The Garonne Lounge was luxurious beyond words. Deep-pile carpeting, brocaded chairs, a cocktail bar and a buffet. Mr Norman, the Aston Villa scout, sat just inside the door. He got to his feet and introduced himself. They sat down in a more secluded part of the lounge. A waiter approached and they ordered coffee and sandwiches.

'We've to meet a few other clubs, too.'

Mr Norman smiled. 'I know. I hear they're outside, queueing in the car-park.'

Gavin sat uneasily in a gilded armchair, the soft French background music doing very little to settle his nerves. He was glad Mr Mooney was present to advise him. There would be plenty of pitfalls ahead, of which he would be unaware. Mr Mooney had told him to take no firm decision regarding his future until he talked matters over with his parents.

Mr Norman was doing all he could to entice Gavin to Aston Villa; he was too big a fish to let go. If there had only been one club in with an offer things possibly would have been more relaxed. But it was obvious that once the big London rivals – Spurs, Arsenal and London Albion – were involved that they would fight particularly hard to land Gavin with as attractive an offer as possible.

Mr Norman left without any decision being taken. He asked Gavin to let him know what he intended to do.

Mr Mooney called the waiter and ordered more coffee. He looked at his watch. 'There's another due in five minutes – Arsenal this time. I've staggered the interviews. Half an hour each, and then out. They'll probably cross paths in the foyer.'

Like clockwork the remaining scouts arrived separately, and put forward their cases individually.

Mr Mooney kept on interrupting. 'Give a date and bring the kid over, let him look around.'

'We'd rather commit him now.'

'What about the trial, then?' reminded Mr Mooney.

'We'll waive the trial. Sign him as he is once he talks the matter over with his parents.'

'What kind of signin'?'

'Apprentice.'

'But he isn't sixteen yet.'

'But he will be in August.'

'How do you know that?'

'We took the liberty and checked it out.'

'I suppose you checked other things too?'

'Yes, and all to do with football.'

Things were moving too fast for Gavin. Mr Mooney took over the negotiations, to the visible annoyance of some of the scouts. Gavin just hoped they wouldn't all get cold feet and pull out of the deal.

'Any chance of giving him a professional contract?' asked Mr Mooney.

'No chance, he has to be at least seventeen, and if we want we can hold out until he is eighteen.'

'Well, we all know that. But just because we all know doesn't mean it can't be done.'

'You mean an under-the-counter agreement?'

'Yes, somethin' like that.'

'That would be illegal.'

'Still doesn't mean it can't be done.'

'No, the club wouldn't allow it. There'd be trouble. No, I couldn't go along with that.'

'You know what you've got here,' added Mr. Mooney.

'Yes, a kid who'll make it if he puts his mind to it.'

'You've got one of the hottest properties ever to come out of Ireland. His like only comes along every thirty years or so. He's worth the best deal he can get.'

'Not at sixteen. Let him come over and look around. If he likes what he sees let him sign in August as an apprentice. When he turns seventeen he can look for a professional contract. Either that or we have an option to hold a kid until they're eighteen before either signing or letting him go. That's the way it works for all kids.'

'All Irish kids, you mean.'

'No, all kids.'

'I could take you up on that.'

'How?'

'The best from England and Scotland always get under-the-counter deals.'

'I wouldn't know anything about that.'

Mr Mooney paused and smiled. Then he came out with a real knock-out punch, the deal scouts did not want to hear about when dealing with fifteen-year-olds. 'Let him wait until he is eighteen. Let him wait until he is old enough to sign a professional contract. Then if you want him you can pay him the money he's worth, not the peanuts he'd get as an apprentice – always with the prospect of being thrown on the scrap-heap after two years rather than getting a professional contract.'

The scout turned to Gavin: 'What do you want to do, kid? There's truth in what your manager said. There's truth, but if you wait until you're eighteen we might lose interest. We'd probably mark someone else. You're dealing with the biggest club in England here. And they don't mark time for anyone, especially fifteen-year-olds. What do you want to do?'

'I'd like to talk it over with my parents. I'd like to have a few days to think about it. Then maybe go over to England. There are four other clubs interested too.'

'I know.'

'I'd like to maybe have a look at the set-ups, think it over and make a decision.'

'We'd go along with that.'

'Set a date then.'

All the interested clubs were prepared to sign him without a trial. There would be a few days with each club. Then in mid-August, soon after he turned sixteen, he was to notify the respective clubs as to his acceptance or otherwise.

The talks in the Garonne Lounge had lasted all morning. When they were over Gavin could hardly wait to get back to Ireland to tell his parents the good news.

Before they left Mr Mooney said, 'I think I'll treat myself to some French cuisine. What are you havin'?'

'Nothing. I'm too full of coffee and sandwiches.'

'Waiter! Waiter! A large vodka and red for me. And an orange for the *garcon*. We're celebratin'. The kid's goin' to sign for Manchester United next season.'

'Why Man United?' asked Gavin.

'Because I support them, that's why.'

'I'm a London Albion supporter myself.'

'Don't let that fool you. Come on, drink up. We've a plane to catch.'

Jimmy Byrne wasn't exactly over the moon at the idea of Gavin becoming an apprentice footballer.

'It's tough over there.'

'But Da, I mightn't get the chance again.'

'Let him go, Jimmy.' Gavin's mother was speaking. 'It's what he wants.'

'Let them come back when he's eighteen. Most kids of

his age don't make it. It's too big of a gamble. Forget about it.'

'But he's always dreamed of going to England. He's put so much effort into trying to be a good footballer. Let him go. You've no right to kill his dream.'

'I won't kill his dream, but England might. It's a different world over there. I didn't spend fifteen years over there workin' not to know different.'

'Da, this is different. This isn't buildin' sites. We're talkin' about the likes of London Albion and Manchester United. Irish players always played for them. They were always well looked after.'

'Yeah, there's the glamour. There's the money. But what's under that? There's the failure. The disillusionment. Right, there's big money, but there's also rejection. Things might be better now but in the bad oul' days . . .'

'You're forgetting one thing, Jimmy . . .'

'Let me finish. In the bad oul' days when there was no freedom of contract an' the maximum-wage, players were only treated like dirt. An' I bet sixteen-year-olds are treated the same way to this day. They ain't got no contract. They haven't a leg to stand on.'

'Jimmy,' Gavin's mother interrupted again. 'You're forgetting a few things. It isn't the money, that's if he's lucky enough to make the grade. It isn't the hardship. It's the fact that he wants to be a professional footballer. It's the only thing he's ever wanted. And now he's a chance of realizing that dream. Are you going to take it away from him?'

'No, but I aim to talk sense.'

'Da . . . if you like . . . we can talk it over with Elaine Clarke's father.'

'What's he got to do with it?'

'He's an ex-professional. He knows what it's all about.'

'So that's who's been filling your head with all these notions.'

110

'No, Da. I always wanted to be a professional footballer. You know that.'

'It's all right dreamin', but there comes a time when that kind of stuff has to be faced. Gavin, this is a big decision. It could shape the rest of your life. Maybe for better. Maybe for worse.'

'What do you want me to do, Da? Not go? If I don't go what am I goin' to be – a builder's labourer?'

'There's no need for that.'

'Da, it's not that big of a decision.'

'You facin' up to me.'

'No, just saying what I feel.'

'Jimmy, forget what he said.'

'Why should I? He's facin' up to me.'

'Jimmy, just forget it, for peace sake.'

'Right. I'm a reasonable man. We'll talk over this reasonably. Got this Mr Clarke's number?'

'Yes, I've got it.'

'Ring him. Ask him to come over some night an' we'll discuss the whole thing. I'm only tryin' to do you right. Understand?'

'Yes, Da.'

'I'm not goin' to see anyone makin' a muck-rake of my son. Even if it's Man United, Arsenal or whoever.'

'Can I ask Mr Clarke over on Wednesday night?'

'Wednesday night's okay. Say eight, if that's okay with him. How's his girl getting on with the runnin'?'

'Fine. She's runnin' in a big race on Sunday.'

'Wish her the best of luck.'

'I will.'

On Wednesday night they saw Mr Clarke. He spelt out the pros and cons, the likelihood of Gavin making the grade or not. Most apprentice footballers didn't. It would be a hard slog; it would take determination and application. There could be homesickness. There could be set-backs. There would be the strangeness of living in England, of having to readjust to the rigours of professional football and stand up for himself in a world of uncaring adults. There was the problem of entering a man's world and being led into bad habits. He'd have to be the judge of his own morals; there would be no one to protect and shield him.

Going away from home wasn't easy for any fifteen-or sixteen-year-old. Going to a foreign country made it even more difficult. And if things didn't work out, it could scar his attitude to football and put him off the game. Even worse, it could sour his whole attitude to life and turn him into an unemployable drop-out.

It was a big decision, one that should not be taken light-heartedly.

'Do you still want to go?'

'Yes.'

Mr Clarke smiled.

Hopefully Gavin would be one of the few lucky apprentices who, eventually, would make the break-through into big-time professional football.

A week later Gavin was gone to England to have a look around and make up his mind as to which of the five English League clubs he wanted to join.

Before he left he had a good chat with Hammer, filling him in on the latest up-dates from the cross-channel clubs, and, more importantly, his feelings about the ones that had made him offers. If Hammer felt despondent he didn't allow it to show and spoil Gavin's barely contained excitement at the prospect of the new life opening up before him. But when Gavin had gone, he wondered to himself if he had taken the right road. Was the Railway Field to be the graveyard of his hopes?

In the end Gavin decided to sign for London Albion, a few days after his sixteenth birthday. The club flew him and his parents over to London for the signing, which was completed in one of the upstairs offices of the club. His father, who now seemed completely won over to the idea of Gavin becoming a professional footballer, felt even more chuffed than Gavin.

Once, years ago, when he worked on the buildings in London, he and a friend were walking past the main entrance of the club around about dinner hour one Saturday. The first team were away from home; there was a reserve fixture down for 3 o'clock. A car pulled in. Two women got out, two of the catering staff. They went through the main door and absent-mindedly left it open behind them. Curious, Jimmy Byrne and his friend walked in to have a look around. They were amazed at the magnificence of the hall. The walls were marble. A massive staircase, twice as wide as a terraced-house, had an impressive display of trophies behind glass casing that extended right up to the top. The pair of them innocently walked up the staircase viewing the trophies. All of a sudden they were stopped in their tracks.

'What are you doing here?'

What were they doing there?

'What are you doing here?'

'Looking at the trophies, of course.'

An athletically-built man in a track-suit stood just above them on the staircase.

'You can't walk in here off the street.'

Jimmy Byrne recognized him. He had been dropped lately off the club's first team. He had a reputation of being something of a hardman. Seeing he was wearing a club track-suit he probably was on the team-sheet for the reserve match later in the afternoon.

'You can't just walk in here off the street. Get out!'

Neither of them said a word. They just turned around, walked back down the stairs and out into the street.

Now, twenty-five years later, he was back with his son. It had taken twenty-five years to complete the journey to the top of the stairs. The doors to London Albion were open to him now, and this time there was no aggressive hardman to tell him to get out.

The signing was scheduled to be in a hotel, but Gavin asked to sign at Brompton where the stadium was. He thought it would bring him luck to sign in the actual place where he was to play his football. A photographer came into the office to record the moment. They wanted to do a feature on Gavin for the following week's match programme, and send a few photographs back to Ireland for the national newspapers. One was to hang for a lifetime in Gavin's family home, right where his father could show it off.

When the signing was completed the manager showed them around. The whole place was impressive, the sense of awe impossible to describe, especially standing out there on the famous pitch. Gavin knew it would be a great occasion if he ever made it to the first team. It would be some honour to play in front of the home-team faithful.

They were booked into a hotel that night and went on the town, courtesy of Gavin's new club. Next day he separated from his parents and was taken to digs where he was to room with a Scottish and a Northern Ireland apprentice. But first he was brought to the club's training-ground where he had his first session with the Youths team squad. He felt a little uneasy. He found it hard to concentrate, but after a while, once the ball was produced and they played a short match, he began to settle and he felt reasonably okay.

Later that afternoon he met up with his parents, but he had to go back to the digs for the night.

Next day his parents went back to Ireland. Gavin was alone for the first time in his life.

9

About the time when Gavin was playing in Bordeaux, Jake was asked by three shady musicians in their twenties to perform at a gig in Greystones Rugby Club. They were part-time musicians who played the pub and wedding-reception circuit. Jake accepted on a once-off basis; he just wasn't into that kind of mediocrity. Greystones was beginning to get him down. The music scene wasn't alive enough. Pretty soon it would be time to look around elsewhere and rope in his own band, a band capable of making an impact – a band that played his kind of music.

Then there was the nagging he was getting at school. The teachers were always picking on him because of the way he dressed. They didn't like long hair. They were never done pestering him to wear a school tie, a standard jumper – even a blazer. He was totally fed-up with all the hassle. School wasn't exactly Jake's favourite place.

The gig in the Rugby Club went reasonably well – until two detectives walked in. They pulled the plugs on the amplifiers and confiscated all the band members' musical instruments, except for Jake's.

'We've been led to believe,' said one of the detectives, 'that these instruments are stolen property.'

'Rubbish!'

'They're part of a consignment stolen from a Dublin warehouse four months ago.'

'We've got receipts.'

'More likely bookie's dockets. Hand over that guitar.'

'Not on your life. I paid for this.'

'Where? In a back lane?'

'No, in Pigotts in Dublin.'

'Produce a receipt within seven days. Otherwise you'll get a summons for handling stolen property.'

'I can't produce the receipt. The dog ate it.'

The detectives left with the band and their instruments. Jake was left to play solo.

It was a wonderful gig. Simply wonderful.

Luke had joined the Bray Invitation Pigeon Club just a month before Christmas. He had bought a racing-clock, and the birds which he had been given by Des Keogh were all paired up. The club had issued him with rings which were to be put on any youngsters he bred, for registration and identification purposes.

The first youngsters, known as squealers, were born about the middle of March. At first they were crop-fed, but after about three and a half weeks they no longer needed to be fed. They were out of the nests, picking at pigeon grain. Luke was told to move the parent hens at this stage; otherwise they would continue to feed the youngsters and delay their independent feeding progress.

Next, Luke began to handle them so that they would become used to the routine. When they were five to six weeks old he introduced them to the sputnik trap, and then, at ten weeks, let them around the neighbourhood, before bringing them off, at sixteen to eighteen weeks old, on training tosses of five, ten, fifteen, twenty, and twenty-five mile distances.

Another part of the pigeons' early training was to rattle a feeder tin to get them to come into the loft quickly. This was achieved by rewarding them with a tit-bit.

By June Luke was well prepared for the pigeon-racing season. But he only intended to race in the young bird races, and they didn't start until July.

He expected to do well.

On the 8th of July Luke waited for his first pigeon to come home from the young bird races. He had locked up all the others in advance so they wouldn't be a nuisance. Some sheets were hanging out on the clothes-line. He removed them in case they would frighten the approaching pigeons. Luke began his watch at half-eleven. At twelve he began to feel agitated. Everything seemed to be strangely quiet, as if the world had come to a standstill. All his attention was focused on the sky.

He saw a bird. It was approaching the loft. He felt elated, right to the pit of his stomach. It wasn't quite close enough to make out if it was one of his pigeons. Then it came closer – and swept to the left; it was a magpie. He was feeling very nervous, very edgy.

He looked again at his watch. Twenty past twelve! His pigeons should be back! Maybe they weren't coming! Maybe they had got caught up in high-voltage wires and were injured. Maybe a hawk got them. Maybe they were just not up to the race and had dropped out. The tension was almost unbearable.

His mother came out into the garden. 'Run down to the shops for me.'

'But the pigeons are coming in.'

'They're comin' in this last hour. It'll only take a minute or two . . .'

Only take a minute? It would take at least ten minutes and, if the shops were full, twenty minutes.

'Ma, I'll go down soon as the first bird comes back. It won't be long now, only a few minutes.'

God, his mother could be a drag. Go down to the shops and if the pigeons came back he would lose valuable time by not being able to grab the first one home and clock it.

'Why can't one of the others go?'

'They're all out.'

Brothers and sisters all over the place – and not one to be found when wanted. The shops could wait.

He began to sweat. Then he saw his first bird coming home. It was definitely his pigeon. It came straight in. For

117

a second he thought it was going to perch on the open water-tank on the roof of the extension at the back of the house. But it dropped straight down and went into the sputnik. Luke rushed into the loft, grabbed the pigeon, took the rubber ring from its leg, put it into a thimble and put the thimble into the clock to record the time.

As soon as he clocked the bird the anxiousness flowed out of him. He still felt excited, but was a lot more relaxed. There would have to be a few rules drawn up. No washing on the clothes-line on race day, no messages to the shops, and the open water-tank on the roof would have to be covered over in case incoming pigeons would fly on to it for water and so lose time. He was learning fast.

Another pigeon came in, and another. Then he went down to the shops and did the messages for his mother. He could hardly wait the few hours or so before bringing the clock into the club in Bray to see how he had fared.

But he was in for a disappointment. His first pigeon home had finished well down the field. But he wasn't too despondent. There was always a next time. He was bitten by the pigeon bug. It was in his blood now, and he would never give it up. Anyway he was learning all the time; getting plenty of advice from Des Keogh.

One day he walked around the side of Bray Head, along the Cliff Walk, to see the Northern Ireland pigeons racing back north from Wexford. They always swept by the shoulder of Bray Head, between that and the outer, lower down, cliffs that jutted into the sea below the railway tracks. It was a warm summer afternoon. The sun dazzled in speckles off the gentle bob of the summertime wavelets. Linnets, greenfinches and rock buntings flitted among the brambles and the headlands of gorse and ferns, above the bare rocky sea-slopes where the gulls perched, hovered and screeched. At the point where the railway went underground into a tunnel, where solitary walkers liked to rest and stare out at the sea and the rocky teeth of the cliffs, Luke paused. He had a pair of binoculars with him.

Briefly, he saw Elaine in the distance. He watched through the binoculars as she jogged into view around a bend in the path. But she quickly veered off to the left on to the track that led over the top of Bray Head. Luke thought of shouting to her but decided not to; he didn't want to interrupt her training routine. In a way he was glad she hadn't noticed himn. He wasn't very good at socializing, especially when it came to talking to girls. He was a poor mixer – more of a loner. He couldn't help it, it was just the way he was.

The pigeons were beginning to appear. They were flying low, almost hugging the lower mountain slopes as if they were afraid to fly over the open water of the sea. The first birds flew in formation past Luke, only feet overhead. They swerved and dipped with the contours of the mountainside. Another flock came over, and another. Luke walked out on to the prickly table of headland above the railway tunnel and looked southwards through the binoculars, scanning for further flocks of pigeons.

The main flock swished over. It was like a large broken cloud, full of movement, full of the different colours of their plumage. After it had passed, the flight passage of the pigeons broke back into smaller groupings. Some of the latter held tired birds that came down on the rocks and the mountain slope; others circled about the mountain, flagging and tired, to drop exhausted among the gorse, the charcoal of the burnt slopes and rocky cliffs to rest, feed and gulp a trickle of rain-water where it lay trapped in small depressions.

By now the birds which were flying over were really worn out. A hawk hovered overhead. It was bent on snatching one. Luke watched through the binoculars. The hawk was high up, almost level with the top of Bray Head. Luke kept the binoculars focused on it. It was dark, with a

119

whitish neck and a barred underbelly. He was certain it was a peregrine falcon. A small group of pigeons struggled tiredly into the shadow of the mountain. The hawk prepared to swoop, its claws outstretched. It plunged at speed, its wings tipping upwards as soon as its claws tore into one pigeon's back. There was a burst of feathers, but somehow the pigeon slipped from the hawk's talons and fell headlong into the ferns, about a hundred feet up the mountain slope from where Luke was standing. The hawk continued on an upward swoop and snatched a different pigeon. This time the bird didn't escape.

Luke scrambled up to the pathway and raced through the ferns and gorse until he got about twenty yards up the slope. There in a patch of beaten ferns he found the injured pigeon. Its neck was ripped and there was a gash in its underbelly. He picked it up. Its eyes opened narrowly, then closed. Its beak seemed to shiver. Although its wounds were horrific it wasn't bleeding much. He took a handkerchief from his pocket, wrapped it around the pigeon, opened his shirt and placed the bird inside. He walked quickly into Greystones, where he got some antiseptic powder in a chemist's shop. Back home he sterilized one of his mother's sewing needles in boiling water and stitched the bird's wounds. He then left it in a quiet corner of the loft and hoped it would live.

Within a month the bird was up and flying again, but flying to Luke's loft. He made a note of the ring number and got in touch with the South Road Federation, which contacted the Northern Ireland Federation. Two weeks later Luke got a letter from the pigeon's owner. The bird was valuable and he wanted it back. He would pay Luke's fare to Portadown.

Luke brought it back one Sunday. That Sunday in Portadown was to change the entire course of his pigeon-racing career.

10

London Albion trained at Highfield, about twenty miles from the main stadium at Brompton. The facility was a big park, with approximately six football pitches and an indoor training area with recreational amenities such as table-tennis and snooker. Without leaving their training base they had the added benefit of going on tough cross-country runs. The apprentices trained every morning from Monday to Friday, and usually for an additional hour on two afternoons per week. Normally they trained on their own, away from the first and second teams. They had their own manager and separate coaching staff. The football and the training were very professional, very enlightening. They were coached in all aspects of the game – skills, tactics, formations. And the glamour was never very far away. Often they got glimpses of the first team players, very occasionally they would play ball with them.

The Youths played in the South East Counties League, while the reserves played in the Football Combination. The fixtures didn't always clash, thus giving a Youth with potential a chance to be given a run on the reserves to see how he could cope with wily teak-hardened professionals. Most of the Youths' matches were played at Highfield and not at Brompton. There were usually only a handful at the matches – no more than the backroom staff, and perhaps a few friends of the players.

Gavin's digs were in Islington. His two room-mates were Sandy Black and Keith Jardine. Sandy was from Belfast. Keith was from near Aberdeen. They were new at the club, just like Gavin.

'What part of Belfast are you from, Sandy?'

'Sandy Row.'

'Sandy from Sandy Row' appealed to Gavin. Not that he had ever heard of Sandy Row. But because of the rhyming effect.

'Sandy from Sandy Row.'

'What y'a mean?'

'Sounds funny.'

'Naw, t'aint funny. You go to Sandy Row and say that. Y'll find out how funny it is.'

Sandy liked to talk about football. He was football crazy. He had great yarns. Keith, for his part, was much quieter. He was a polite, sensible type of person. But you could see that he was homesick. He didn't really like London, although their landlady, Mrs Burtinshaw, did everything possible to make him feel at home.

Each morning they were picked up at the end of the road by a private bus contracted to London Albion to bring the Youths to Highfield for training. There were several other pick-up points along the way. The bus-ride was always high-spirited, but nothing really wild – nothing that would get out of hand. London Albion had a very strict code of discipline. It was impressed on them that any boy who didn't conform would get his marching orders.

Their trainer, Bill Thornbull, was a fitness fanatic. He ran them over every square inch of Highfield.

'This is worse than the black taxis back in Belfast.'

'What's the black taxis?'

'Sometimes you don't come outa them alive. Jus' like Bill's trainin'.'

Bill wasn't a football coach as such; he hated the sight of a ball. He was an athletics coach. He loved to run the apprentices into the ground, revelled in seeing their suffering. An ex-army man, the bullying nature of the army always came out in him. He had a way with the apprentices – his way. Nobody would be sending him any Christmas cards.

The gym was his second home. He loved pumping iron. He had all the apprentices on weights – not body building but weight training. 'There's a difference,' explained Bill. 'Weight trainin' will increase your speed and all-round strength. Light weights combined with runnin' will work wonders.' Out came the stop-watch. He had graphs for each player. Compared their sprint times every week. Put them on special diets. Checked their body weight. They sweated, they ached, but their times improved. They became quicker. 'Fleet of foot,' as Bill put it.

'Fleet of foot 'n' mouth,' muttered an apprentice.

'What's that you said?' Bill rounded on him.

'Nothin'.'

'Are you from the country?'

'No, I'm from Brixton.'

'Well, any more remarks like that an' you'll end up on Dartmoor with a twenty-pound pack on yer back and a banana sandwich for company.'

Then there were the football coaches:

'Strike the ball this way.'

'But I can't.'

'Eye on the ball. Pivot. Make contact with your instep. Follow through.'

'But I can't do it that way.'

'You can. It's all about technique.'

Football coaches were a pain in the neck. And when they started blackboard tactics . . . It was worse than going through a geometry session.

'4-3-3. What's that?'

'It's the area code for a betting shop.'

'Who said that?'

Silence.

The door opened. Bill Thornbull stepped in. 'Eaves-droppin' is a favourite hobby of mine. Come on, lads, misdemeanours must be punished. Six laps of Highfield.'

Early on, during their first week with the club, the

apprentices were asked if they wanted to study. A man came in from some college and handed out leaflets. He gathered them all after training and asked if they wanted to continue with their school education, study for a profession, or learn a trade.

'I want to study accountancy.'

'I wanna do a course on business studies.'

'I wanna do a trade. Carpentry.'

'What do you want to do?'

'I don't know.'

'And what do you want to do?'

'Nothin'.'

'You can't do nothing.'

'Wanna bet?'

The man left. Gavin decided to study for his A-levels in his spare time. If nothing else it would kill a few hours. The year before, he had got good grades in his Junior Certificate. The one moment he would never forget from that series of exams was during the geography paper when Rasher Murphy had whispered over to Gummy Davis, 'What's the capital of Russia?'

'Moscow.'

'Spell it.'

'M-O-S-S-C-O.'

After a week of Highfield training they were brought to a quiet seaside town where they ran along the beach and up every sand-dune in sight. They did either six-mile runs, eight-mile runs or ten-mile runs every morning. In the afternoon they did short, snappy, circuit-training in the grounds of a local college. In the evening they were allowed out to relax or walk along the Promenade. But they had to be in their rooms by ten-thirty. It was during those walks along the Promenade that Keith, Sandy and Gavin got to know each other better.

'I don't think London's right for me,' murmured Keith. 'I think I'll ask to go home.'

'Don't. If you do you might never get another chance.'

'I wouldn't mind. Rangers wanted me. They might still take me.'

'Back in Belfast, Linfield asked me to sign,' said Sandy.

'Who's Linfield?'

'The poor man's Rangers. The best team in Northern Ireland.'

'They're Protestant, aren't they.'

'Aya, that's why they're best.'

'Same wi' Rangers. You're Catholic, Gavin?'

'Yeah. So what?'

'Nothin'. Jus' wonderin'. I've a few mates back in Aberdeen who're Catholic. Doesn't make much difference.'

'Does in Belfast,' said Sandy. 'But maybe that's bein' different just for the sake of causin' trouble. We can walk along here and there's no aggro. You wouldn't do it in Belfast.'

'Why not?'

'Maybe it's somethin' to do with being British,' said Gavin off-handedly. He didn't give a tupenny fig about Northern Ireland. 'Maybe if you thought of being Irish first there wouldn't be so much aggro.'

'Strong words.'

'Listen, Sandy. I don't give a damn. And if you were smart you'd think likewise.'

'Suppose you're right. But Northern Ireland should be about people, not politics. It's the workin' class that's sufferin', not the politicians. An' the sooner you down South realize it, the better.'

'Sorry, Sandy. Let's talk about something else.'

'Like what?'

'Like Aberdeen.'

Those few days at the seaside seemed to have a settling effect on Keith. He came out of himself, was more talkative, didn't mention going home so often.

At the weekend they played a match against local opposition. The going was tough. Because London Albion was a big name club the opposition packed their team to the hilt with the pick of the local senior talent. But in the end London Albion ran out handy winners at 3-1. But Bill Thornbull wasn't satisfied. He thought they were very sluggish in the first half. He had them up first thing Sunday morning doing a stint over the sand-dunes. It was sheer hell. In the end the Youths were glad when the time came to go back to London. But Gavin was as determined as ever to stick it out. He knew that even with education his job options would be severely limited. He knew in his heart that his best chance of making it in life was through football. In a way this seeming lack of opportunity helped him to get over the periodic bouts of homesickness he felt during his early days in London. This was his one big chance in life and he had to take it. There was virtually nothing else.

His friendship with Keith and Sandy continued to grow. Sometimes late at night they would open the bedroom window, climb down the drain-pipe, and go to a nearby cafe to sit and drink coffee and play a few video games. The fact that they were never caught had to be attributed to sheer good luck, and the fact that none of the neighbours had dogs that barked when the dustbins began to clatter.

On Saturday nights they were allowed to stay out until 11.30, and Gavin usually brought the two lads to the Irish Club in Kilburn for a night's entertainment. The journey back to the digs was always thought-provoking. Just outside the Tube stations, and on some of the streets, they saw numerous shapes flopped down in shop doorways and in the archways of alleyways; the shapes of kids not much older than Gavin, wrapped in cardboard and newspapers, settling down to sleep for the night. They were mainly Scottish and Irish, with a few English. They had all come to London, either looking for work or because they had run away from home. They were all destitute, too young to claim unemployment benefit, too proud or too troubled to go back home. They were a grim reminder that all was not right in the world, and that it was very important to keep on the straight and narrow.

After a few Saturday nights of passing the 'cardboard streets', Gavin, Sandy and Keith got sense and gave up climbing out of the bedroom window and going to the cafe. They were afraid that if they got caught they would end up like the unfortunates sleeping in the streets.

Life at the club wasn't too bad for the apprentices. They heard stories about other clubs where it was almost traditional for apprentices to clean boots, sweep terraces, and do all kinds of menial tasks which had nothing to do with football. But Gavin and the other apprentices at his club didn't have to do anything like that. It was an entire football education; and everything revolved around football.

One famous story always going the rounds was about the way a London club from one of the lower divisions treated two apprentices. They were signed on and immediately handed paintbrushes and cans of paint. They had to paint the entire stadium, from the stands to the crush-barriers to the flag-poles. When the job was finished, either that or when the paint ran out, the two apprentices were let go. They never got to kick a ball. Whether the story was true or false Gavin was not sure. But he was inclined to disbelieve the maliciousness of the details.

Another story, unfortunately true, served as a warning to Gavin and all the other apprentices and professionals that should they ever get homesick they were not to leave without first getting the club's permission. The season before, a young Northern Ireland player had signed professional forms with a London Second Division team. He left his club without telling anyone, went back to Belfast and signed for a junior club in another name. A

127

protest went in against him, and it was upheld. The London club heard what happened and lodged a complaint with the Irish Football Association; the player was under contract and had broken the terms by turning out for another club. The Irish FA heard the case. They issued an ultimatum: Either the player go back to London, or face suspension for the remaining three years of his contract. He refused to go back to London, was banned for three years and had to sit out a vital period in his footballing career, missing out on gaining international caps at U-21 level.

Gavin was determined that there would be no such complications in his career. And indeed homesickness was less of a problem than he had feared. He and the other apprentices were all very well treated. London Albion had only one expectation of the Youths' team for that season – that they give a good account of themselves in the FA Youths' Cup.

Luke took the train to Portadown on the first Sunday in September with the rescued pigeon. He was met at the station by Arthur Irvine, who drove him to his house in a housing estate on the outskirts of Portadown. There were UVF slogans all over the place. Luke felt jittery. Having introduced Luke to his family. Mr Irvine took him out to the loft.

The loft was immaculate. Luke had never seen anything like it before. Mr Irvine showed him his top birds and explained what they had won – seemingly he was one of the top pigeon men in Northern Ireland. He checked the bird Luke had brought back, and Luke explained all about the hawk and the attack.

'He's in marvellous condition. I wouldn't have thought he could have survived such an attack. And wouldn't, except for you. All my fault, really. I shouldn't have raced him . . . not that race. He was over-raced. Needed a rest.'

Luke told him how he was doing with his own pigeons. Mr Irvine gave him some words of advice and a few tips. It was all new to Luke. He had heard none of it before. Then Mr Irvine gave him a present of a bird as a reward for having nursed the injured pigeon back to health.

'You'd pay big money for a bird like that,' said Mr Irvine. 'That bird I wouldn't sell for less than three hundred pounds. I'm giving it to you for a few reasons. Now I'm telling you something else. Here's an address in Belgium. Write to it and give my name and the ring number of the hen I've given you, an' you'll get a cock that, when bred off my hen, 'll do well . . . very well, much better than many an experienced racer ever did.'

'What would the cock cost?'

'A hundred and forty pounds sterling. But mention my name and you'll get it for seventy pounds sterling.'

'I'd be murdered if I spent seventy quid on a pigeon!'

'You're a pigeon man, aren't you?'

'Yes.'

'Well, it's worth it then. The hen will be paired with the right cock. You'll thrive. Breed for next year and race the youngsters end of season. You won't regret it. You've seventy pounds, haven't you?'

'Almost.'

'Well, get the rest quick as you can. Save!'

'I'll think about it.'

'Do it.'

Mr Irvine asked him inside for dinner, where he was welcomed by Mrs Irvine, a small, bright, friendly woman, with a habit of cocking her head to one side which reminded Luke of one of his livelier pigeons. There were two sons. William, the elder, was about Luke's age. He gave him a rather sullen glance and didn't take much part in the conversation which, mainly conducted by Mrs Irvine, was safely about the weather, holidays, the garden – Luke had been impressed with the immaculately kept lawn and the riot of roses everywhere, comparing it guiltily with the beaten-down patch at the back of his house where only weeds seemed to flourish.

The younger son, Jeremy, kept giving Luke curious glances. It made him feel embarrassed.

Then during a lull in the conversation, Jeremy said out of the blue, 'You're from the South.'

'Jeremy . . .'

'The bogey-man's from the South. He brings bombs from there and kills people.'

Luke felt uneasy. He was thinking of the UVF slogans on the walls outside. 'I don't know about that.' All of a sudden the atmosphere had become very strained. It wasn't easy having to sit there facing the Irvine family.

'The bogey-man never sleeps at night. He goes around killing Mammys and Daddys. I hate the bogey-man.'

'Jeremy, Luke is a guest.'

'Isn't it true?' William gave Luke a hostile look. 'They want to kill us all. They started it in 1641 . . .'

'1641?' repeated Luke, trying to resurrect some dim historical facts. 'There was a rebellion. The Irish rose up against the English, I think. Or was that Cromwell?'

'The Catholics rose up against the Protestants. They killed them all.'

'I never knew that,' said Luke in amazement. He was about to add that they couldn't *all* have been killed but thought better of it.

'It's true, more's the pity,' said Mr Irvine soberly. 'Here in Portadown, hundreds of men, women and children were driven into the river. Just because they were Protestants. Anyone that escaped was clubbed or shot to death.'

'Why don't we change the subject?' said Mrs. Irvine and there was silence for a while. But when she went out to the kitchen Mr Irvine leaned over to Luke.

'You mustn't be offended. It's nothing personal. But you

grow up with that here in Northern Ireland. You're lucky you don't have to face the strain we're all under. It's hell having to face pressure from the paramilitaries – on both sides. Maybe people down south would understand us more if they saw us as families, as flesh and blood, not as a tradition, a piece of land to be fought over. We're law-abiding people and we're getting bombed and maimed and the people of the Republic don't seem to care.'

'But we do,' said Luke. 'We hate the violence.'

'In the border areas farmers are being exterminated just because they own a parcel of land. The politicians put us into this mess and now they can't get us out of it. You saw the UVF slogans on the walls outside. Next thing they'll be in the people's hearts and we'll all be finished. Not just Northern Ireland. But the South as well.'

Luke didn't know what to say. Luckily he didn't have to make the effort. Mrs Irvine came back with apple-pie. Shoe shot a warning glance at her husband.

'Jeremy is interested in pigeons too,' she said.

'Yes . . . I've one of my own. His name is Scout.' Jeremy spoke with a touch of pride. 'Sometimes he follows me to school.'

'What kind is he?'

'A fantail.'

Luke was feeling more at ease now but underneath he was still in a state of shock. Could what Mr Irvine said be true?

After dinner Mr Irvine drove Luke, his three hundred pound pigeon in a box under his arm, back to the station, put him on the train for Dublin, and waved him a cheery goodbye. On the journey back south Luke concentrated on his pigeon plans. He thought long and hard about what Mr Irvine had said and about buying the Belgium cock. Could he do it? He could! If he made sacrifices he'd have the balance of the seventy pounds within a month. He'd make it somehow. Make it and tell no one, especially his parents.

He just hoped he wasn't making a fool of himself by spending seventy pounds on a pigeon. Had he known it, it was to be one of the smartest moves he was to make in his entire life.

A month later, the balance of the money saved, he sent off to Belgium for the cock. It was sent over and held in quarantine for a time. Luke brought it home, put it in his loft and never said a word about it to anyone.

That was another piece of advice Mr Irvine had given on that Sunday afternoon. 'Never tell anyone your business.'

When Luke came back from Portadown, he was interested enough in what had been said at dinner to look up 1641 in his sister's history book. 'Tales of massacre and wholesale slaughter of settlers spread to England,' he read, 'and were accepted as genuine.'

Maybe they had different history books up in Northern Ireland.

He was to hear from Mr Irvine again. He wrote some time later, wanting to know how Luke was progressing. Luke wrote back and from that day on they corresponded on a regular basis. Mr Irvine sent a generous amount of information and advice, telling Luke how to race and train over the various distances, emphasizing the importance of correct diet, special vitamins, the gradual build-up of training distances, keeping accurate records of the pigeons' times in the training tosses. When put into practice it was much more successful than the advice he was getting from Bray. Even his old birds improved.

Luke would be forever grateful to Mr Irvine, as pigeon men normally didn't divulge the secrets of their techniques. But he was really pinning his hopes on the following summer, when he would have the new stock bred off the Portadown hen and the Belgian cock.

There were so many races to look forward to – the

Young Bird Skibbereen National, the Young Bird Penzance National, Youghal, Barley Cove, Valencia, Dinard, Oak Hampton, and the King's Cup from Rennes in France.

The year would pass quickly.

Elaine was beginning to make a name for herself with Crusaders. But it was only with the coaches – the inside experts; the general public knew very little about her. She was competing in 'open' competition against seasoned runners, finishing fifth or sixth, or maybe as low as tenth in a field of fourteen runners. But her times were improving. She was getting down to 3.05 in training for 800 metres. Her cross-country times were reasonable too. Within a year she expected to get down to 2.93 for 800 metres. After that the sky was the limit. She was one to watch for the future: very quick over the last two hundred metres and tactically aware. She was prepared to bide her time.

One Friday night she met Jake at a 'live' gig in Bray. She was with some of her school friends. He was on his own, studying the band, getting an idea what the competition was like.

'How's it going, Jake?'

'Not bad.'

'Care to join us?'

'Not them. They're all snobs.'

Elaine wasn't put out. Jake was Jake. One took him as one found him.

She left him to himself and went back to her friends.

Shamrock Boys and Hammer started the U-16 season playing in Dublin. The U-16 section of the League had fallen through in Wicklow – not enough teams had entered – so under rule Shamrock Boys were allowed to play in the Dublin Schoolboys League, for that season at least. It was Sunday football, mostly 11 o'clock kick-offs. Within six weeks most of the players, including Mousey Burke and

Robert Smyth, were losing interest. They were finding it hard to get up out of bed on a Sunday morning. Usually they met as early as 9 o'clock to get into Dublin for kick-off. A lot of the players were out late on a Saturday night, which meant that the manager had to go to their houses and knock them up. That, coupled with the fact that they were losing most of their matches, meant that interest in the team was on the decline.

But not so with Hammer. He was always at the pick-up point on time. And his form never slumped. If anything he was getting better and stronger all the time. He was a treat to watch. He always wore his jersey outside his knicks, with the sleeves rolled up, the knicks hung low about his hips, almost as if they were about to fall off. It was one of his idiosyncrasies. But there was nothing sloppy about his play. He was a gem, a real thoroughbred, who, when it came to stroking a ball about, or making a tackle, or marshalling a defence, looked the complete master. And although Shamrock Boys at U-16 level were doing badly Hammer's form was certainly noticed. From playing on the pitches beside the high-rise flats in Ballymun, where a 'Mister Sheen' aerosol was tossed from a balcony by a careless housewife and just missed the Shamrock manager, to the plushy environs of Bushy Park on the southside, Hammer was watched with more than a passing interest. The Irish U-16 selectors were showing an interest. They sent out representatives to watch him play. Some of the local League of Ireland clubs also noted his name for future reference, intending to give him serious consideration when he turned eighteen.

But, though Hammer showed good form, Gerry Horgan was worried. He was beginning to lose heart, not so much with the number of matches they were losing, but because most of the players were becoming more interested in girls, and that was the reason they were staying out late on Saturday nights.

He called a players' meeting. He was blunt and scowling. 'I'm fed up with the lot of you. I'm fed up havin' to chase after you. Always having to remind you what time to meet, having to go round to your houses and try to knock you up out of bed – and half the time you don't even bother answerin' the door to say you're not comin You're getting one more chance and that's it. Get it?'

The slightly stunned players pledged that they would change their ways. Cross their hearts. There would be no more absenteeism; they would all be there on the Sunday morning – on time. Never again would the minibus pull away without them.

But after two weeks players began to go missing again. They only had ten two weeks in a row. Then it was down to nine. Then back to eleven. The following week they only had eight. That did it! Gerry Horgan had had enough. He told the club secretary to inform the League that they were pulling out.

Hammer was disgusted with the so-called friends who had let the team down by not showing up for the matches. The team had been together since they were nine and now it was finished, because some of the players were no longer interested, and were too lazy to put in the effort to keep things going.

For a full week he didn't think about football. He didn't train, just sulked. He wondered if he should go and talk to Mr Clarke, but what good would that do? He had warned him this could happen. So had Elaine.

One night as he sat brooding, a knock came to the door. It was the man who managed St Joseph's in Sallynoggin.

'I hear your team broke up.'

'Yeah.'

'What do you intend doing?'

'Don't know.'

'Play for us?'

'What about trainin'?'

'Come down to Sallynoggin one night a week. Other than that, train on your own.'

'What about matches?'

'I'll pick you up in Bray and leave you back afterwards. Is that okay?'

'Suppose so.'

'You'll come down for trainin' Thursday, won't you?'

'Yeah.'

'If you like we'll sign you there and then and inform the League. You should be able to play within two weeks. Will that suit you?'

'Suppose so. Anyway, the way things are nobody else has asked me to sign for them. Thanks for makin' the offer.'

'The pleasure's mine. See you Thursday, then?'

'Yeah, see you Thursday.'

The man went back to Sallynoggin and Hammer made his way there the following Thursday. He signed after training, but didn't play until the following Sunday week. As his old team had broken up he automatically became the property of the League, and clearance had to be granted before his transfer became valid. The League discussed the transfer in council that Monday. They informed Hammer's new club that he would be eligible to play from Sunday onwards. It was a good move for Hammer as his new team were top-notch and played in the 'A' section of the Dublin Schoolboys League. But Hammer couldn't but feel sorry for Horgan. The poor man had lost Gavin, but that wasn't too bad, at least Gavin had progressed and made a name for himself. Now he had lost Hammer, and all because some of the more mediocre players in the team had lost interest. Only two really first-class players had ever been produced by Shamrock Boys – Gavin and Hammer – and now they were gone, headed towards fame and stardom; gone just as surely as the team which spawned them was catapulted into oblivion.

11

Stevie Hodgson was the manager of London Albion Youths' team. He was an ex-professional who played for the club in the Seventies; he had been a fringe player, playing most of his football on the reserves. The club had sold him off to Reading in his mid-twenties. When he finished League football he got an FA coaching badge. London Albion asked him back as Youths' team manager. He jumped at the chance. Mind you, he had no qualifications to manage – his qualifications were in coaching. But London Albion believed he was just the man to motivate the apprentices and Youth team players.

First match of the season was at Highfield. London Albion v Holborn in the South East Counties Youths Division.

'We've got to win this one, lads.' It was Stevie talking. He was wearing a green and white London Albion track-suit. First match of the season, sets the pattern. Who're Holborn?'

'Cobblers,' said one of the London born apprentices.

'Correct,' enthused Stevie. 'Cobblers every time. We've got tradition on our side. All Holborn's got is cobblers. Who's the best?'

'London Albion.'

'Keep it that way, lads.'

There wasn't much room in the dressing-room. Not that it was small. But quite a crowd had squeezed in. There was always a lot of interest in the Youths for the first match of the season. Many of the club staff had come down to have a look, give the players a quick one-two over, and then go. They wouldn't be back unless the team put in an exceptional run in the FA Youths' Cup. That was the way it was year in year out.

Gavin was handed the number 9 jersey. He was to play up front with a black player, Darren Blyth. Darren was a big lad with some second-team experience. He was in his last season at Youths' level. London Albion used him as a target man, and Gavin had built up a good understanding with him during the pre-season fare of friendly matches. The players had a nickname for Darren, 'Cocoa', which he didn't mind in the least. London Albion was family. But if opposing teams called him 'Cocoa' he would try to get in with a headbutt when the match officials weren't watching. Darren was very good at using his head. But it was a talent that London Albion didn't appreciate.

Sandy Black was playing right-full.

Keith left-full. And a gem of a player, it must be said.

Then there was the 'Ealing Terror'. He was the anchor-man in midfield. Mick Bates was his name. He was as hard as nails. One tackle and he owned the ball. He was brought up hard and played hard. His father was an ex-professional with Millwall at Cold Blow Lane. Mick could play the ball about and dictate the trend of the game.

Then there was Glenn Thomas, a Welsh kid, who played centre of defence, and Cyril Stevens, his central defensive partner. Cyril was from Devon, and he had an accent akin to Long John Silver's. But he had two good legs. A shot in either foot. It would have been no bother to him to play centre-forward. He was adaptable. But centre-half was his regular position. He was an English Youths' international. Gavin, Sandy and Keith were the only U-16s on the panel. The rest were all U-17s with the exception of Darren Blyth and the goalkeeper, Colin Baker. They were in line to have a very strong Youths' side the following season as only Darren and Colin would have to be replaced.

'Get out there on the pitch, lads. You've had enough in trainin'. See how it goes doin' the real thing. Get to it, lads.'

They trotted out on to the pitch. Holborn were already there; they had their backs to London Albion. Mick Bates went up for the toss. Not a word was spoken. The two captains just glared at one another.

London Albion won the toss.

Bill Thornbull, the trainer, was on the line. He was wearing a suit. He had just come from doing the shopping with his wife and he hadn't bothered to change into a track-suit. Stevie Hodgson was pointing a finger, admonishing him.

Holborn got stuck in straight from the kick-off. They harried and chased. The pitch was very dry, very hard. The ball wasn't holding up. They really had it in for the 'Albinos'. Mick Bates had to remind them of his Millwall heritage. He set out to teach them a lesson, and show them how to play football. The referee had to take him to one side. 'Now, Mick. Now . . .'

Then it was 'Now, Gerry. Now . . .' with the Holborn mid-field dynamo. Nobody was bothering Darren Blyth up front though. They were all afraid of his prowess with the head.

Then the Holborn manager went into a huddle with his coaching staff. 'We can beat this lot.'

'How?'

'Mike Bates controls the midfield. The team that controls midfield usually wins, right?'

'Right.'

'Well, this is what we'll do. Tell Jamie Tyler to go in hard on Bates. Do it a few times. Bates'll retaliate. With a bit of luck he'll be sent off.'

'But Jamie'll be sent off as well.'

'It'll be worth it. With Bates off we should win the game.'

'But, Boss, that wouldn't be fair.'

'Who cares? It'd be great to give London Albion a beatin'.'

'Anything would be worth that.'

'Well, do it then.'

The message was relayed to the pitch, and not without sophistication.

Five minutes later there was an incident involving Mick Bates and Jamie Tyler.

Three minutes later there was another incident. The referee produced two yellow cards.

Four minutes later there was bedlam. Mick Bates had lost his cool and flattened Jamie Tyler. He was sent off.

The Holborn management was as pleased as Punch.

Somewhere along the line Gavin came into the picture. Keith Jardine went on a run down the flank. He played a one-two and cut inside and let fly with a low curling shot just inside the bottom upright. The goalkeeper got to the ball. It spun off his fingertips back into play. Gavin was very quick to follow in and touch the ball over the goalkeeper's sprawled body into the back of the net.

'Who's he?' asked the Holborn manager.

'Don't know.'

Later on in the game Gavin got a second goal from a knock-down by Darren Blyth. He hit it on the volley with his left foot. He usually didn't score many goals with his left foot. But the power of the shot gave the impression that he was capable of scoring at will with his 'other foot'.

'Did you find out who your man is?'

'He's some Irish kid.'

Come full-time London Albion had won 2-nil.

The Holborn manager said to one of his coaches, 'Put you in a bad humour, wouldn't it? Bad enough gettin' beaten by London Albion. But when the Irish give it to you, that's the pits. Remember Colm Maguire?'

'Him that played centre-forward for Holborn years ago?'

'His father or grandfather was Irish. He ended up hittin' one of his own players in a League match. Don't talk to me about the Irish . . . And as for London Albion . . . It

140

couldn't have been worse, except maybe if Cocoa Blyth had a scored."

'You can say that again.'

'He turned us down. Wouldn't sign for us as an apprentice.'

'I know.'

'Said we weren't good enough.'

'Some day we'll teach them. We'll show them. Holborn'll be kings of Europe.'

'Yeah, when Colm Maguire's grandsons are playin' for us . . .'

During the opening weeks of the English League season Gavin, Keith and Sandy got to see a lot of Premier and First Division matches. At that time of year there were always midweek matches, mostly on Tuesday and Wednesday nights.

The games were a real treat for the three lads. They got to see all the top London teams: Arsenal, Spurs, Chelsea, West Ham, playing at Highbury, White Hart Lane, Stamford Bridge, Upton Park. And there were the other London clubs: QPR, Crystal Palace, Millwall, Charlton, Leyton Orient, Wimbledon, Fulham. The lads had a good look around enjoying every minute of it, the sights of London, the trips on the Underground, all the football chatter to and from matches, discussing tactics and star players.

Sometimes they would talk about teams from their own part of the world.

'Shamrock Rovers. Where're they from?'

'Dublin.'

'Shelbourne?'

'Dublin.'

'What's your team, Sandy?'

'Linfield. They play out of Windsor Park.'

'Where are Carrig Rangers from?'

'Carrickfergus.'

'Glenavon?'

'Lurgan.'

'Distillery?'

'Belfast.'

'What about you, Keith? What team do you follow?'

'Rangers.'

'What about Aberdeen? You're from there.'

'Near there. They're good. A lot of good players played for Aberdeen.'

'What do you think of Chelsea?'

'Has beens.'

'Tottenham?'

'Good club. Good set-up. Haven't got the killer instinct though.'

'What y'a mean?'

'Their players are too soft.'

'Man United?'

'It's not football that matters up there. It's money.'

'It's goin' that way with a lot of clubs. Television callin' the tune. They set the fixtures.'

'They're entitled to. They pay the money, don't they?'

'I've a good chance of gettin' a call-up for the Northern Ireland Youth squad this year,' beamed Sandy.

'Hope you're lucky. I'll have to wait. The Scottish squad is too strong for a sixteen-year-old to get into. I'll be happy enough if I make it in two years time. Wha' about you, Gavin?'

'The Republic's squad is strong enough. Not too strong though. I should make it next year.'

'What'll we do tonight?'

'Go to the pictures.'

'What's on?'

'The Return of Holborn.'

'What?'

'I'm only jokin'.'

'Good. Let's get ready.'

Although the Youths didn't get to mix a lot with the full-time professionals at the club there still was a certain amount of contact, mainly at training level. Most of the professionals were internationals and the Youths held them in awe. The main reason the two segments didn't mix was not because the professionals were big-headed about their status, but more because the Youths had not quite progressed to adulthood and that, of course, left an obvious chasm, especially at a social level.

But leaving awe, international caps and star rating aside, the Youths, from their disadvantaged standing, still got a laugh from some of the stories that would filter through the grapevine about the stars of the club.

One concerned a player who ran half the length of Brompton with his knicks torn off and nothing on underneath. He scored a goal on the occasion. But the referee disallowed it, citing ungentlemanly behaviour. His decision nearly caused a riot.

A recently departed first-team left-full could nearly always correctly forecast the results of all the games he played in. His name was Jason Digby – a seventh son of a seventh son, or so he said. He proved something of an embarrassment to the club. If Jason gave an unfavourable forecast against London Albion the players knew in advance that it was hardly worth their while to make an effort to win the match. Instead they would just go through the motions and save their energies for a more favourable day. He was bad for club morale and was quickly transferred to QPR. But he brought good luck to them. They prospered, as did the Shepherd's Bush betting fraternity.

Then there was the second-team player who never quite made the grade. He was lazy, so lazy that sometimes he sent his identical twin to play in his place. London Albion got fed-up with his antics half way through the season and transferred him to Brentford, who weren't quite sure if they had got him, or his twin . . . or both.

All that apart, playing for London Albion was a very serious business. There was no room for messers.

The man involved with the day-to-day running of the club and the manager of the first team was John Warner. Regarded as the shrewdest manager in the Premier Division, he had a good track record and had taken London Albion to two League titles in four years. He was a typical hard-working Scot, always around the first team, keeping a sharp eye on the reserves. There were no favourites with him and when an unpleasant decision had to be taken he took it; there was no shirking responsibility.

As for the Youths, they had to ferment – be given time before they would merit his attention. Apprentices like Gavin wouldn't come to his personal attention until it was time to be retained as a professional, or let go. But although the Youths didn't see much of him, he knew exactly what was going on and how they were progressing. He had files on all the players. If there was ever trouble, or if an apprentice was unhappy for one reason or another, John Warner was never slow to react and the door to his office was always open, for better or for worse. He wasn't the best manager in the English League for nothing.

In spite of her dedication to athletics, Elaine missed football. Now that she was no longer playing she realized that there was a void in her life. Sometimes on a Saturday she would go to the Railway Field and see how Shamrock Boys were getting on. She began to take an interest in the younger teams. Maybe on a Tuesday night she would go down and help with training. She never saw Hammer because he was now playing on Sundays and on Sundays she was tied up with Crusaders. But she heard about his team's break up.

She was glad when he decided to play for St Joseph's of

144

Sallynoggin. He deserved to be with a good side and St Joseph's was a good side. She wrote and told Gavin about the break-up of Shamrock Boys U-16. She knew Hammer was unlikely to mention it. Although he loved football he never talked about it.

Gavin's old team manager from Cambridge Boys had approached Elaine to join a girls' team in his locality. Although strongly tempted to sign she declined. She had made up her mind to concentrate on athletics and in her heart she knew she couldn't serve two masters. But she could never quite get rid of her yearning for soccer. One day a class-mate, Sally, asked her over to Cornelscourt to play in a kick-about with a ladies' team that played league football. The name of the team was Brighton Celtic. Sally was English-born and, like Elaine had only come back to live in Ireland recently. She had played for Fulham Ladies and was no mean performer. Neither were the Brighton Celtic players. They were impressed with Elaine and wanted her to join, but she declined. She hesitated over her reply though. The club secretary felt it would be only a matter of time before she would change her mind.

A few weeks later Sally asked Elaine back to Cornelscourt for a friendly match. She went and played really well. The Brighton Celtic crowd were ecstatic.

'Why don't you sign?'

'I'm committed to athletics. I couldn't do both.'

'But athletics is more a summer thing.'

'All the preparation and all the hard slogging is done in the winter. I just wouldn't have time.'

'Listen, women's soccer needs quality players. With a few people like you playing people would be inclined to take the game seriously. The sport is badly in need of star performers. Don't turn your back on football. Soccer needs you.'

'I'll think about it.'

'Sign for the Cup then. That won't hurt you.'

Elaine signed, but with the stipulation that she would only play in the Cup.

'There's just one problem,' said the club secretary. 'A player has to play a minimum of two League games before she is allowed to play in the Cup.'

'Well,' answered Elaine. 'I guess I'll have to play in two League matches.'

The Brighton Celtic club manager smiled contentedly. She had got her man . . . sorry . . . her woman.

One Saturday afternoon Elaine was coming back on the Dart with school friends, after playing a hockey match in Sandymount. Jake was on the train. He was wearing a leather jacket and had a guitar-case on the seat beside him. He said 'Hello' to Elaine. A few of the girls, including Elaine, sat beside him. The rest were just across the aisle.

'Girls, this is Jake,' said Elaine. 'He thinks you are all snobs.'

'Does he? What is he, a queer?'

Jake felt mortified. He didn't know which way to look. All around him there were girls giggling and laughing. And Elaine Clarke was having the best laugh of all. He couldn't wait for the train to get to Bray station so he could disappear from their sight.

'And they're supposed to have manners,' he thought darkly.

London Albion Youths won their first five fixtures. They were on a roll. They beat Bournemouth, Brentford, West Ham, Southend and Luton. Then they were due a tough away game to Spurs – a North London Derby game. Training was stepped up a little more that week. They were brought together with the reserves for a practice match. John Warner even had them brought in to Brompton to give a hand to clean up the terraces and the dressing-rooms – just to remind them that they were part of London Albion and to take pride in their club. They were even brought into the boot-room to give a hand with the first team's gear.

The match against Spurs Youths, played at White Hart Lane, attracted a sizeable crowd for a Youths' match. It was played on a Tuesday night under lights. Spurs Youths were a good side. Half the team were on professional contracts and had played reserve team football. They were unbeaten and playing the best football in the South East Counties Youths Division.

'Go out there and get to them. Mick, plug the back of midfield. Anythin' that moves close down. Sandy and Keith, support the wide men. Glenn, Cyril, shove tight. Gavin, let Darren take the flak. Be ready for the loose ball and keep probin' for openin's. Darren, for Pete's sake keep your cool. Lose the ball, cover back. Pick 'em up as quickly as possible. That includes you, Gavin. Okay, get out there.'

They were greeted with a boo by the crowd. The Spurs cockerel was crowing.

'Tot . . . en . . . 'am! Tott . . . en . . .'am!'

The London Albion back-up team, plus the two substitutes, took up positions in the dug-out.

'Come on, ye Spurs!'

Gavin could feel the adrenalin going. There was a touch of atmosphere at White Hart Lane.

'Cocoa . . . ! ugh . . . ! ah . . . ! ugh!'

The Tottenham diehards on the terrace behind the goal were slagging Darren Blyth. He paid no attention, just blasted a shot over the bar in the kick-about before the match, in the hope that it would bounce off one of the loud-mouths.

'Cocoa is a nana . . .! a . . .! ah . . .! ah . . .! ah.'

'Come on the Albinos!' Bill Thornbull roared.

The referee blew for the kick-off at 7.15. The first ten minutes was all Spurs.

'Tott . . . en . . . 'am! Tott . . . en . . . 'am!'

147

Glenn Thomas and Cyril Stevens were holding down the centre of the defence admirably. Keith and Sandy were doing a good job in the full-back slots. Mick Bates was holding firm in front of the back four, closing down everything and taking hold of the ball in an attempt to slow the game down and take the momentum out of the Tottenham attacks. Mick was some player – some player.

After twenty minutes Tottenham hadn't scored. Their slick passing movements began to falter.

London Albion began to come into the game. Mick Bates began to dominate the midfield.

'Come on the Albinos!'

Then one of the London Albion midfielders went on a run. He played an angled pass to Gavin. Gavin dummied the centre-half and squared the ball to Darren Blyth. He picked his spot and let fly. Spurs 0, London Albion 1.

Darren didn't let the occasion go unmarked. He rushed in behind the goal and shook his fist at the Tottenham crowd. The referee cautioned him. And as he was doing so Darren gave the crowd the two-fingers, unseen by the referee and the linesmen. The crowd really bayed for his blood after that.

Sadly, though they played well, London Albion lost 2-1. Spurs were top of the League, unbeaten after six matches.

In the dressing-room Stevie Hodgson tackled Darren.

'Darren.'

'Yes, Boss.'

'I saw that.'

'What?'

'You givin' the crowd the two-fingers.'

'They were slaggin' me.'

'It's conduct unbecoming. You shouldn't have shook your fist at them neither.'

'Boss, I ain't a pair of football boots. I got feelin's. They were slaggin' me.'

'Doesn't matter. London Albion won't tolerate that kind

of behaviour. We've a reputation to live up to. Your kind of behaviour sullies that reputation. Darren, I'm sayin' nothing about this. If I did you could be in serious trouble with the club. Know what I mean?'

'Yes, Boss.'

'So as to teach you a lesson I'm leavin' you out of the team for the match at Plymouth. I hope you learn. I don't want any more of that kind of thing from you. Understand?'

'Yes, Boss.'

Darren understood. But it wasn't clear whether he had learnt his lesson.

The players changed, went outside, got into the team bus. They would hear plenty about losing the game when training at Highfield the next day. To lose against Spurs was always a bitter pill to swallow.

Tomorrow Gavin had to go to school for a few hours. Life was turning into a daily routine. At last, playing for London Albion had become an everyday occurrence. Gavin, Keith and Sandy had settled in.

Elaine played her first match for Brighton Celtic in the Ladies' Dublin District League on the last Sunday in October. It was a home fixture at Cornelscourt against Lakeside. The League was due to close down in a few weeks for the long winter break and Brighton wanted to make sure Elaine would have her two compulsory matches played well before the Cup campaign began.

In the pavilion before the match Elaine began to feel nervous. Apart from Sally she didn't know anyone. Most of the girls were a lot older than her. One was an Irish international, and talk had it that there was another international among the opposition. They could hear the Lakeside pep-talk coming from the other dressing-room. The sound of football studs clattered off the concrete floor. Someone was bouncing a ball off the visitors' dressing-room wall. Outside, on the pitch, there was a drizzle.

It was a dark, murky day. The ground was soft, curls of muck in the goal areas. Lakeside looked as if they meant business. They ran out on to the pitch in single file, a ball to every three players. They broke into groups and tipped about, waiting for the referee to get proceedings under way.

Elaine, down to play midfield, gave a quick eye over the pitch. The surface looked reasonable enough – no pot-holes. The goal areas were slightly submerged due to the lack of grass. That meant that the cross-bar would be that few vital inches higher than normally expected. She looked to see if the Lakeside goalkeeper was big or small. She was smallish. The sunken goal areas would be a definite disadvantage for her, especially if a few shots were directed high into the corners.

Elaine found the going a lot tougher than she expected, especially after her long lay off. At first she found it hard to think quickly football-wise; to move the ball, create space for herself. But the longer the game went on the more she found the old skills coming back. The pace of the game was a lot quicker than when she played schoolboy football for Shamrock Boys. After half an hour she latched on to a through ball. She accelerated straight for goal, taking the Lakeside defence by surprise. She calmly side-footed the ball into the net, to the left of the goalkeeper. Brighton were 1-nil up.

Lakeside retaliated. Two lightning quick goals.

In the second half the tempo upped, mainly from Lakeside. But they were wary of Elaine. She twisted and dodged. Chipped the keeper, hit the cross-bar. She nut-megged one of the fulls and sent a low cross to the back post. But there was nobody there to take advantage.

Then with ten minutes to go Lakeside scored a third goal. They had the cushion of a two-goal advantage. But they didn't sit on their lead. They scored a fourth goal. Finally, with only seconds left, Elaine went on a run. She squeezed past two defenders and sent a rasping shot across the diagonal of the penalty area straight into the top corner of the net.

Not bad for a sixteen-year-old.

'Who's she?'

'Elaine Clarke.'

'Where have you been hiding her?'

'One of the girls brought her down a few weeks ago.'

'She's a good one.'

'You can say that again.'

Elaine Clarke had made an impression. Within two months of the League starting up again after the winter break she would be well known around the environs of ladies' soccer.

A new star was born. And ladies' soccer needed as many stars as possible.

On that same Sunday, Hammer's new team, St Joseph's, played Cambridge Boys in a home League fixture. Cambridge had lost two other players apart from Gavin to cross-channel clubs during the close season. But they were still the top team in the Dublin Schoolboys League. They beat St Joseph's easily enough.

After the game, a few of the Cambridge Boys players approached Hammer.

'You Gavin's mate?'

'You made a mistake not signin' for us. You coulda been in England by now.'

'How's Gavin gettin' on?'

'We don't hear much about him. Our manager says it could take four years for him to make the breakthrough.'

'Next time you write, tell him we were askin' for him.'

'Tell him Skinner Hayes wants to nut him.'

'Who's Skinner Hayes?'

'Our number 9.'

12

Jake was walking down Greystones one Thursday afternoon. A man came up behind him and tapped him on the shoulder.

'Take the team Saturday?' asked the man.

'What?'

'Take the team Saturday?'

'Why?'

'I'm goin' away for the weekend. Take the team?'

'Who're they playin'?'

'Wicklow.'

'What age?'

'Under fourteen.'

'Any transport?'

'Yes, minibus, meetin' at the Railway Field ten-thirty. The players all know.'

'Is the minibus paid for?'

'Yes, I'm payin' tonight.'

'Make sure you do. Do I take subs from the players?'

'No, I'll look after that when I get back.'

'What about the kit?'

'I'll leave it up to your house tonight.'

'What about the referee's card?'

'The players can tell you their names, you can fill it in.'

Jake walked on down the street. A match Saturday. Such bliss! Manager for a day! All his old enthusiasm for football flared again.

Friday came and went. Saturday dawned. It was to be a red-letter day in the annals of the League Disciplinary Committee.

Jake was outside the Railway Field at 10.30. So too was

the minibus. But there was no team. Fifteen minutes later there still was no team. The players mustn't have been told. Either that or they had got their days mixed up.

The fixture! Jake thought hard. Give a walk-over? No way! Get a team. Keep a cool head. All you have to do is get a team together.

Jake got into the minibus, and they drove off in the direction of a housing estate. Two lads were walking down the road.

'Get your gear.'

'We don't want to go.'

'Get your gear.'

'What's it under?'

'Under fourteen.'

'We're fifteen.'

'Get your gear. It doesn't matter.'

'Can Harry come?'

'Who's Harry?'

'He's our mate.'

'What age is he?'

'Sixteen.'

'Yes, get him. I'll meet you at the bottom of the road in five minutes.'

The minibus moved on. Jake got out and knocked on a door.

'We're playing a match. Coming?'

'What kind of match?'

'Soccer.'

'I'm a rugby player.'

'Doesn't matter. You've a phone. Ring a few of your pals and tell them to meet us at the bottom of the road in five minutes.'

'How many?'

'As many as you like. You can bring a whole scrum for all I care.'

Back on the road, Jake kidnapped two ten-year-olds who

had their football gear with them. They were on their way to play an U-10 match at the Railway Field.

'Mr. Smith'll go bananas if we don't show up. He'll go mad.'

'I'll go madder. Shut up and get in.'

The two frightened ten-year-olds did as Jake commanded. They got in and the minibus drove off to the bottom of the road to wait and see how many players fortune would bring them.

Eight players showed up. That, along with the two ten-year-olds made ten players. They were one player short.

'Never mind,' said Jake to the driver. 'Drive on. I'll play myself. I'll play in goal and let the other team hump it.'

They got to Wicklow in time. Played the match, and won 2-1. But there was trouble The referee reported Jake for ungentlemanly behaviour. Worse, Wicklow lodged a protest and won. They lodged it on the evidence of the referee's card, on the grounds that the players listed were unregistered with the League, and over-age.

Jake, in his humour, had filled the card in thus:

1. Packie Bonner
2. Sinead O'Connor
3. Elvis Presley
4. Mick McCarthy
5. Jack Charlton
6. Harry Looper
7. Granny Smith
8. Denis Law
9. Bobby Charlton
10. Wicklow County Council
11. George Best

Jake was never asked to take charge of a team for Shamrock Boys again. And his name was put on the League's black-list. But, like the saying goes: He died a happy man.

Luke decided to make early preparations for the breeding season. He was expecting great things from the Portadown hen and the Belgian cock. He gave them pride of place in the pigeon loft – a completely separate section where they wouldn't be disturbed. He paired the rest of the birds up in the general section of the loft.

First he'd have to think about bringing the pigeons into breeding condition. There was a special conditioning mix for doing that; Haith's Red Band, plus a Breeding Mix that was new on the market. He also bought some hemp, not too much. This he fed sparingly to the cocks so as to make them rank. He began to feed the hens extra grit so that they wouldn't lay 'soft' eggs. Then he had to see that he had enough nesting-bowls and tobacco stalks to line the nests with. Tobacco stalks were recommended instead of straw so as to cut down on lice and parasites. Pigeons were prone to mites and had to be treated periodically to prevent an accumulation. Also, the loft had to be disinfected and sprayed with a lice-killing liquid before the breeding s eason commenced. Lastly, the pigeons had to be dewormed. It took Luke a month to prepare for the breeding season, but by the New Year he had all his preparations made. His big hope was for some quality youngsters off the Portadown hen and the Belgian cock..

It was an anxious wait.

Elaine played her second match for Brighton against Rathfarnham. Then the winter break came. The ladies' league closed down in November and wasn't due to open again until the end of March.

Her athletics coach wasn't too happy about her playing soccer.

'Most women's soccer is played in the summer,' she said. 'It could interfere with your racing schedule.'

'But I'm only playing in the Cup. The Cup doesn't really get going until September.'

'You'd still have a few races in September. Suppose you got injured playing football?'

'I won't.'

'All it would take is a sprained ankle. It could put you out the very weekend there'd be an important race.'

'It won't.'

'I've known it to happen. You can't serve two sports.'

'It's only a few Cup games.'

'I'm not happy about it. I'd prefer if you didn't play at all.'

'I promised I'd play.'

'Have it your own way. But it's not the right decision.'

Elaine understood only too well her coach's concern. But she had enjoyed her two games with Brighton Celtic. She couldn't see why playing a game or two could do any harm. There would only be a few games in the Cup – only one if they got knocked out in the first round.

Anyway Elaine was looking forward to the summer race meetings; the Cup games were months away. She was hoping to get down to 2.85 for the 800 metres. She was even contemplating running 400 metres for a while to build up her speed.

She still went on runs along the Cliff Walk and over Bray Head. Sometimes Hammer went with her. The talk naturally was about the other three. Gavin sometimes wrote to her, always about football.

Jake was almost completely obsessed with the idea of becoming a rock musician. He wasn't seen about much, and rarely without his guitar. He was usually on his way into either Bray or Dublin, trying to make contact with this guy, this band, gigging in different people's homes, comparing techniques and experimenting with various guitar heads he had come into contact with.

As for Luke: It was just pigeons with him. Sometimes Elaine would come across him out along the Cliff Walk. Seemingly he was always on the look-out for pigeons. She thought him a little odd. He was hard to talk to, never said much, and the only thing he seemed to be interested in was pigeons. He was a real loner, difficult to get to know. Maybe that was a challenge!

She felt sorry for Hammer, though. He was a really good footballer. But so far he had gained no real recognition, no major representative honours. She could see it was getting him down slightly. But he was putting on a brave face. She hoped things would happen for him soon. He deserved some success.

Things weren't going too well for Jake at school. The only solution was to change schools. So after Christmas he enrolled at the Community College in Bray. He settled in quickly. Some of his class-mates played on a local soccer team and asked him down to train one night. Because of the ill-starred expedition of Shamrock Boys U-14 to Wicklow he was *persona non grata* in Greystones so he was only too glad to go for a kick-about and some training in Bray, even though it meant having to get the bus into Bray and not getting back home until fairly late.

The team trained on Bray Promenade. They togged out in one of the shelters and always played an hour's football on the grass between the flower-beds before going off on a run along the Prom.

They weren't the only team that trained on the sea front. Lots of teams trained there. They turned the lawns bordering the Promenade into a quagmire. The matter was brought to the attention of the Town Council and an immediate ban was put on teams playing on the sea front. But Jake's new team were a stubborn lot; they were the one team that refused to give in. Anyway they had no place else to play football on a winter's night. The shelters, although not cosy, were adequate for changing in. And the big plus was the street lighting which illuminated the grass lawns they played on. More than anything they needed the lighting. No, they were not going to move, even if it meant being caught by the police and fined in court. They intended to stay put and defy the Council's warning to prosecute. One or two of the players took turns to act as sentries during training sessions and if a squad-car approached, a whistle would be blown and the whole team would grab their clothes and disappear.

But the best fun of all was when the caretaker for the sea front arrived on his Honda scooter. He was always well wrapped up winter and summer, and wore an impressive helmet and goggles. The team called him their trainer, and they used to run around Bray, with him chasing after them. They always escaped by eventually splitting up and hiding in gardens and back alleys.

The fun and games didn't last for long. The Gardaí finally caught up with them and warned them off, and that was the end of football teams training on the sea front.

But Jake's contact with the football team was of benefit. Two of the team – Kev and Dave – played guitar, and one day after school the three of them got together and played a few chords. They decided to form a band.

Dave played bass guitar, while Kev played rhythm guitar. Jake played lead. All three of them could sing. Dave and Jake were particularly strong singers. They could front the vocals, while one or the other took turns doing the backing with Kev. Luckily they didn't have to look very far for somewhere to practice. Kev's father owned a factory and he gave permission for the threesome to use a store room at the back of the premises for rehearsals. All the necessary power-points were in place for the band-equipment, and the acoustics were quite good. As it was sound-proofed, nobody was put out by the emissions from the band sessions. In short, the set-up was ideal.

They needed a drummer, and they got one. Liam was his name, from Shankill. He just drifted into their lives. One Wednesday they were in a cafe having a chat and he came over to their table.

'Hear you formed a band.'

'Yes.'

'Need a drummer?'

'Yes. What are you like?'

'Noisy.'

'Good.'

'When do I start?'

'Practice Saturday and Sunday.'

'I'll be there.'

So far they had no gigs. But that didn't worry them. They had no manager either. No cause for alarm. It was early days yet. Everything would come together in time.

What did worry them was – they had no name for the band.

'Think of a name.'

'Sphinx.'

'Too cultured.'

'The Undead.'

'Not enough life.'

'Blue Lagoon.'

'Sounds like a travel agency.'

'Equinox.'

'Sounds like the weather forecast.'

The thinking caps went on again. They just couldn't come up with an acceptable name.

London Albion Youths lost two more League matches before Christmas. League leaders Spurs remained unbeaten.

Sandy Black had got called up for the Northern Ireland Youth squad. But he didn't make the starting line-up. A few weeks later he began to lose form with London Albion Youths and he was dropped. It was a very trying time for him. He felt like throwing the lot in and going back to Belfast. He was called into John Warner's office for a chat.

Stevie Hodgson was there as well. They advised him not to make a hasty decision, that it probably was only a temporary set back. That as soon as his form returned he would feel a lot happier.

'Don't worry, stick it out, son. It happens to the best.'

Then Gavin began to show a loss of form. He became sluggish and tired. Not only that; the goals dried up for him.

Stevie Hodgson talked it over with him.

'Gavin, I'm not worried about the goals. It's the tiredness I'm thinkin' of. You lads gettin' to bed late, or what?'

'No, Stevie. Check with the landlady.'

Stevie checked.

'Maybe it's too much football. We'll rest you a few weeks.'

The few weeks did the trick. Gavin came back into form just in time for the FA Youths' Cup. But the best poor Sandy could do was to make the subs' bench. Not so Keith Jardine. He seemed to be going from strength to strength all the time, getting better and better.

Their first round FA Youths' Cup fixture was against Birmingham City at St Andrew's. All FA Youths' fixtures were decided on aggregate over two legs. It was a tough game. Glenn Thomas and Cyril Stevens were the real stars. But Gavin scored both London Albion goals in a 1-2 win. The home leg at Brompton was a lot easier. London Albion ran out comfortable 4-nil winners.

They then had a run of four League matches. Sandy got a start in one of the games, a home League fixture against Portsmouth. It didn't do much to help his cause. He played poorly.

Stevie Hodgson took him to one side. 'Don't let it get to you. Think positive. Put it out of your mind. Relax, son.'

London Albion blew their League chances in mid-February. They lost three matches on the trot and that was that. Stevie Hodgson wasn't too happy. Neither was John Warner. He called Stevie into his office and gave him hell.

'Three games lost on the trot. Explain.'

'One, bad ref. Two, no luck. Three, Darren Blyth got sent off.'

'What's up with Darren Blyth?'

'A bit of a hothead, John.'

'We've never had disciplinary problems with the Youths until Darren Blyth started. What's going on?'

'Darren's sufferin' from a complex. Thinks people are makin' a laugh of him because of his colour. There's not much I can do about it, John.'

'Send him in to me. I'll have a talk with him.'

Stevie Hodgson sent Darren Blyth to John Warner's office. Darren felt sure he was going to get his marching orders. He hadn't been in John Warner's office since he had signed a professional contract. Nothing much had changed. Still the meticulous neatness everywhere. Still the photograph of London Albion's double winning side.

'We've a problem here, Darren. It's time you and I had a heart-to-heart talk. You've been with this club four years. One on associated schoolboy forms, two as an apprentice, and this year on full professional forms. It's this disciplinary record of yours. What's the matter?'

'Nothin' much, Boss.'

'Now, how many bookings have you had this season, Darren?'

'Five.'

'Sending offs?'

'Two.'

'Darren, you've got to learn to handle yourself. We've all got responsibilities at this club. We are all accountable for our actions, Darren. If you don't curb that temper of yours you'll be in trouble. I have my responsibilities too. I have people t o answer to. And if I have to I will act. So be warned. Get rid of that chip on your shoulder.'

'What d'ya mean, Boss?'

'You've got this complex about being coloured.'

'Nobody's goin' to slag me, Boss, an' get away with it.'

'You're not the only coloured player at this club. Learn to sort yourself out. Don't give those National Front yobos something to crow on. You've got a future, Darren. Don't ruin it.'

Darren left the office. Kept out of trouble for a while. But those nearest to him, Gavin and company, felt it would only be a matter of time before he would fly off the handle again and land himself in more trouble.

In the second round of the FA Youths' Cup London Albion drew Blackburn Rovers. The first leg was at Ewood Park. Blackburn put up a tough struggle. They played hard and direct, typical old-fashioned cup football. There was passion in their play, and they completely knocked London Albion out of their stride. Blackburn had their best Youths squad for years. It almost brought back memories of the glory years before the lifting of the maximum wage. They got a deserved 1-nil victory but were beaten in the second leg. Glenn Thomas scored off a corner and Gavin secured a second goal from a shot by Mick Bates which rebounded off the cross-bar.

London Albion disposed of Stoke, Liverpool and Manchester City in later rounds. They were due to meet Newcastle in the semi-final and that was where their Cup run came to an end. The game at Brompton was a scoreless draw. In the second leg, at St James's Park, London Albion went into a 1-nil lead, courtesy of Gavin. But Newcastle equalized almost from the centre. Then the roof fell in for London Albion. Darren Blyth struck back and floored one of the Newcastle defenders. The Geordie crowd bayed for his blood. The referee gave him his marching orders.

London Albion fell apart, not so much because they were down to ten men, but because they knew Darren had had his last chance. He'd never wear an Albinos' jersey again. Newcastle beat them 5-1 and went on to lose the final, 4-3 on aggregate, to Spurs of all clubs. It was to be the culmination of a fine season for Tottenham: Youths' League and Cup double.

On the way back to London after the Newcastle debacle, everyone was in the dumps. Poor Darren Blyth sat at the back of the coach. There wasn't a word out of him. He knew he'd get the call to John Warner's office in the next few days. He knew he was on the way out. He'd been warned often enough. Now he'd blown it. Some of the lads tried to cheer him up. Others sat moping over the defeat. Stevie Hodgson didn't feel too good either – nor Bill Thornbull. Stevie knew John Warner would shoulder the blame for Darren's actions on to him. After all he was supposed to have control over the players. He only hoped he wouldn't get the sack.

They got back to London about three o'clock in the morning. Next day Darren was called into John Warner's office. He received a club suspension until the end of the season. His professional contract wouldn't be renewed. He would be let go.

Darren knew his reputation would precede him. None of the big clubs would be interested in him. He could forget about English representative honours. Only some lower division clubs would be prepared to take a chance on him. It was almost certain that he would never play for one of the bigger clubs again. He had blown his future.

The players felt sick for Darren. He wasn't even allowed to train with the team. But the tragedy made Sandy Black sit up and think.

'I'm goin' to get my place back,' he vowed. 'I'll come back from Belfast after the summer. I'll stick it out. Darren Blyth's a great player. Look what's happened to him. This is not just about football. It's about character, guts, overcomin' the odds. I'm goin' to fight my own fight. I'm goin' to give it everythin' to get back on the team.'

'Best of luck, Sandy.'

'Save it for Darren, he needs it more than me.'

Someone must have saved Darren some luck. Southend came in for him at the end of the season. They got him on a free transfer. He played superbly for them. Even got to the point of controlling his temper. From Southend he went to Luton. But he never played again for a top club, nor for England. Still, all the fans, sports-writers and players knew he was in a class of his own. When the big clubs came unstuck at Southend and Luton it was always Darren Blyth who did the damage.

'There is only one Da . . . rr . . . en . . . Bl . . . yth! Only one Da . . . rr . . . en . . . Bl . . . yth!'

London Albion didn't win the South East Counties Youths' Division either. They finished fourth. The cupboard was bare at Highfield.

Hammer's first season in the Dublin Schoolboys League finally petered out its mid-table existence. When the evening matches began, St Joseph's were down to play a team at Fairview Park on Dublin's northside. Everything was in a hurry – rushing to get the team together – rushing to get to Fairview Park – rushing to tog out – rushing to fill in the referee's card. It was only at half-time that the referee was handed the match-card. First he checked the two listed teams. Then he checked the front of the card. Trouble! The listed fixture on the front of the card was at variance with the titles of the teams listed inside.

'You St Joseph's?' he asked.

'Yeah.'

'You Sheriff YC?'

'Yeah.'

The match on the front of the card read 'Sheriff YC v Valeview'. St Joseph's should have been playing Belvedere YC. They were both playing the wrong team! In all the flurry before the match the two teams and the referee had taken it for granted that they were playing the right opposition. A few pitches further down two teams had gone home. One was Belvedere YC, the other was Valeview. Both intended to claim walk-overs.

There was another complication; Sheriff YC were a U-15 team, not U-16.

The referee pointed out the error to the two managers. The managers were furious. They blamed the referee.

But really they were all to blame. The match was abandoned. The players only laughed. The referee asked for his match-fee but the two managers, quite rightly, wouldn't pay up. It was a sore point. The matter was reported to the League. As it was an end-of-season game and the fixture had no bearing on the winning of the League it was decided to let it go by the board. It was never refixed. Neither was the U-15 fixture. Schoolboy football was full of such barmy cock-ups.

So ended Hammer's first season in the Dublin Schoolboys' League. The manager was already on the look-out for new players to strengthen the squad. He was preparing for a do-or-die effort the following season.

The big push was on.

Gavin's season ended on a different note.

Stevie Hodgson called him aside the day before he was due to go home. 'By the way, Gavin, the Boss wants to see you in his office this afternoon. Three-thirty. He's got a surprise for you . . . he's goin' to offer you a professional contract.'

'He's what?'

'You're going to be on a contract next August when you turn seventeen. You and Keith are the only younger players offered one. The rest will have to wait to see how they're fixed. Congratulations, Gavin. Next season you'll be a fully fledged professional.'

Gavin could hardly believe his luck.

'You're not havin' me on, Stevie, are you?'

'Course I'm not. It's not part of my job to be taking the mickey out of anyone.'

'That's great, Stevie. Just terrific.'

'Course it is. Me, Bill and the rest of the gang wish you luck. You're a good 'un, Gavin. Just keep at it and never mind the distractions.'

There was a silence. Gavin was thinking of Darren Blyth. He wondered if Stevie were too.

'About Darren. You'll be getting a replacement for him?'

'Why d'ya want to know?'

'I'd be playin' up front with him. I'd like to know.'

'We've a kid from Birmingham in mind. Only thing, he's talkin' to Villa. He's to let us know what he's doin'. With a bit of luck he'll sign for us.'

'If he doesn't?'

'We might switch Cyril Stevens from defence to attack.'

'But that could leave us open at the back. Who'd cover for him?'

'Maybe switch John Palmer from right-full and bring Sandy Black back into the full-back slot.'

'I've a friend, a centre-half back in Ireland. Could you give him a trial?'

'We've a scouting system. We'd have to cover it with the scouts first. They might get annoyed if we didn't. What club does he play for?'

'St Joseph's, Sallynoggin. It's near Dublin.'

'Any representative honours?'

'Not really. He played U-14 for Wicklow though.'

'Sure he's good enough to bother bringing over?'

'I think he is.'

'You would say that, you being a friend.'

'No, Stevie, Honest. He's a real good one.'

That night Gavin couldn't sleep with excitement. A professional contract . . . and maybe Hammer's big chance! He could hardly wait to get home with the news.

13

When Gavin came home with the big news, he was treated like a star. Jimmy Byrne was delighted with him. His mother was just happy that he had settled in so well. He went down to the Railway Field and met all the lads. Gummy Davis, Robert Smyth, Rasher Murphy and all his old team-mates with Shamrock Boys dropped by to see him. All of them had given up soccer, though Robert had joined Greystones Rugby Club. He was more in his element there. His accent fitted in rather better than at the Railway Field.

Hammer congratulated him warmly. Gavin didn't tell him about the prospect of a trial with London Albion. Just in case it fell through.

The day after he came home he went to see Mr Clarke. Hammer came with him. Elaine was there too, keen to get all the latest football gossip and discuss her prospects for the coming season.

A few days later Luke asked Gavin over to look at his loft. He stood there and listened, hardly understanding any of the pigeon terms Luke used, putting up with the cooing of the birds and all the white lime-like powder on the loft floor. Luke showed him his prized youngsters. He was due to race them soon. He picked out a pied cock and said he had high hopes for at least three of his youngsters. Gavin was beginning to get fed up but he didn't let it show. Just another few minutes, and hopefully they would be out of the loft. He felt on the verge of sneezing. But Luke kept going on and on. He began to dose about ten pigeons for a bacterial infection, forcing a tablet down each pigeon's crop. A cupboard just inside the loft door was full of remedies for different ailments – sour crop, one-eyed cold, canker, and a host of other pigeon ailments. The pigeons dosed, Gavin still had another ten minutes of pigeon-related talk to endure.

'I raced last week. I wasn't in the hunt though. But I'm happy the way my pigeons came. I got fifty rings this year and bred forty youngsters. See these two here? I'm hopin' for big things from these two youngsters.'

'How big?'

'I'm hopin' to be up there with the top fliers. Maybe finish in the top six. There's something special about these two youngsters. You can tell. I bred them off a hen a man from Portadown gave me. I'm keepin' them back especially for the top races. I only found out a few weeks ago that the hen the man gave me was bred off a King's Cup winner.'

'What's the King's Cup?'

'It's the top pigeon race in Ireland. It's the BIG one. Gavin, I know I'm goin' to do well with these youngsters. They're goin' to click for me.'

Gavin wasn't over-interested. Pigeons meant nothing to him. By the time he got out into the fresh air he could feel a bout of hay-fever coming on, thanks to the atmosphere of the pigeon-coup. The two of them went down into Greystones to the harbour and sat on the rocks. It was nice and sunny. They lay back and dozed in the sun. Gavin squeezed his eyes shut and thought of taking it easy for the next seven weeks, no more running, no more training, no more squelching through mud in the freezing cold, just loads and loads of sun and cool summer breezes.

Luke thought of his pigeons.

That night Gavin went up to Dublin with Hammer to watch him play in a football tournament. He was sure that the London Albion scout would be there. He hoped Hammer would be at the top of his form.

The following night, Jake asked Gavin to come to a band practice. Hammer and Luke went too. The practice session was in their usual venue, the storeroom of Kev's father's factory. There were bits and pieces of factory equipment in a corner, but the complete top section of the room was taken up with the band's equipment.

Gavin, who thought there would only be the bare essentials, a few beat-up guitars and a second-hand drum kit, was amazed at the mix of amplifiers, microphones and musical instruments. Everything looked top quality. It was evident, from the hi-tech equipment, that the band meant business.

'Where did you get the money for all this?'

'Kev's father got some through sponsorship, and we have to pay the rest back to him as we go along.'

'This is wild. Have you got a manager?'

'We don't really need a manager, not yet. Not until we're good and ready.'

'Have you any gigs lined up?'

'Not really. We' been asked to do a few. But we're not ready yet. Maybe in a few months.'

'How are you going to move all this equipment?'

'Dave knows a fella with a vegetable van. Maybe we'll throw him a few bob. Maybe we'll ask him a favour.'

Jake led Gavin, Hammer and Luke over to the drum kit, took the dust-cover off the main drum, and pointed at the logo on the drum.

'Scorpion Jack . . . That's the name of the band. From Jack Charlton. Right now we feel ready to play public. But we want to work on our music. We got plans. Big plans. We want a certain amount of original music. That's the only way we'll make it. When we have a good mix we'll go public. Maybe in a few months, a year at most.

'Kev's father got a feed-back. Years ago there used to be a beat club in Bray, down at the Albert Walk. Lots of good sixties groups played there – only all their music was copycat. Nothin' original, and they really didn't get anywhere. Well, Kev's father hears the beat club's goin' to open again. Says he'll get us in as a support band and see how it goes from there. He used to play a bit himself – started out with a fellow called Fran O'Toole who lived around the corner from the beat club. Fran was brilliant, played for the Miami Showband. He was getting on well and beginning to write his own music when he and most of the Miami were killed near the Border just outside Newry. Sad case. But anyway, Kev's father's got connections. This rock c lub is going to be big. The top Dublin groups will be all down to play there. And Kev's father is mad keen on this beat club idea. It brings back memories to him. Like I said, he played there as a kid. Says Dickie Rock's brother played there.'

'Who's Dickie Rock's brother?' asked Luke.

'Who's Dickie Rock?' asked Hammer.

'Dickie Rock was big, *is* big. Should have been bigger, like we're goin' to be. Got the message?'

Gavin, Luke and Hammer had certainly got the message.

Jake, Dave, Kev and Liam got in behind their instruments and within minutes, as if an invisible curtain was pulled open across a stage, they began to play. First the rhythm guitarist, then the bass, then the lead, with the drummer fluctuating the beat beautifully.

Scorpion Jack could play music . . . real music . . . rock music!

Elaine's athletic season was in full swing. She had come second in the Leinster Schools Senior 800 metres, and, that for a girl who was giving away two years, was outstanding. Her open meeting times with Crusaders were continuously improving. But her coach wasn't totally satisfied. 'There's room for improvement.'

'Maybe next year.'

'No, I want another two seconds off your time before the summer's out.'

'Two seconds?'

'Yes, two seconds.'

Elaine knuckled down; by the end of August she would knock 2.5 seconds off her best time.

A few days after the Leinster Schools Senior Championships Elaine was walking down Main Street in Bray when she spotted Luke.

'Hi!' she called.

Luke looked around to see who she was calling to. Then Elaine was beside him.

'I mean you, silly. Got a moment?'

'Well, actually . . .'

'Of course you have. I must talk to someone and here you are. Sent by providence. Come and have a coffee.'

'I've no money.'

'I have.' She turned into a coffee shop, smiling over her shoulder at him as he hesitated. 'If I ask you, *I* pay. If you ask me, *you* pay. Simple?'

They sat down in a dim corner and Elaine ordered coffee and cakes.

'I'm at a cross-roads, I don't know what to do. I want some advice.'

'I'm no good at givin' advice.'

'All you have to do is listen. It's the old thing. Soccer or athletics. Athletics or soccer.

'Why do you have to decide?'

'I can't do both. Not if I want to get to the top. I'll be doing my Leaving next year. If I want to concentrate on athletics I should be thinking about the States. Villanova. Like Sonia O'Sullivan . . . You're so lucky.'

'Me? Why?'

'You can race pigeons anywhere. If I want to be a world-class runner, I'll have to go away for training. The same with soccer. I don't want to spend my life in a backwater here. It's a pleasant backwater. But it's a backwater.'

'Like Hammer.'

'Hammer is wasted. And he knows it.'

When she looked at her watch and said she must go, Luke was amazed to find that they had been there for over an hour. To his surprise he found he had enjoyed talking to her.

'I'm afraid I wasn't much use . . . giving advice,' he said as they stood outside on the street.

'You were a great help. I really just wanted to think aloud . . . it wasn't too bad, was it?'

'What?'

'Talking to a girl.'

Hammer appeared around the corner. He seemed nonplussed at seeing Elaine and Luke together.

'Pity you didn't come along sooner. You could have joined us,' said Elaine. 'There I was looking for someone to talk to, and first Luke and then you happen along.'

Hammer's face cleared. 'I'm getting a trial,' he blurted out. 'With London Albion.'

'Fantastic.'

'Tell you what. If you get signed up – and you will – we'll have a party. The father and mother of all parties.'

Hammer went to London Albion for a week's trial. They liked what they saw. He signed apprentice forms. He would begin his career in September – though that would mean he would miss pre-season training. Gavin and he would share digs.

14

The weekend after Hammer came home something happened in the pigeon-racing world that was to be the talk of the fancy for years to come. The same something was to put Luke on a pedestal which would lead to setting him apart from other pigeon men. The occasion was a big Southern Federation over-year race from Dinard in France. Two hours before the first birds were due back a thick, dense fog fell in a line between Wicklow and Balbriggan in the east coast area. The fog was especially thick around Dublin. So thick, in fact, that it brought traffic to a standstill.

Only one bird came home, a grizzle hen bred off the Portadown hen and the Belgian cock. It came gliding down out of the fog and into the sputnik. Luke didn't even realize it was there, not until he stumbled down the garden in the fog, not until he got right up close to the sputnik and saw the shape of the bird inside. He rushed into the loft, grabbed it and clocked the thimble. The fog stayed around for hours. It was too bad to even attempt to drive to Bray. But two days later the word was out all over Dublin and most of the east coast that Luke's grizzle hen was the only bird to survive the fog and find its way home.

At the end of summer, Luke, Gavin, Hammer and Elaine went into Dublin, to one of Scorpion Jack's gigs. Each had something special to celebrate.

The venue for the gig was heavy with a rock world atmosphere. Scorpion Jack rapped out number after number. The lads danced. Elaine danced. The place was hot and clammy and the music fab.

173

'What d'you think of Scorpion Jack?' flashed Hammer.

'Great.'

'They're better than Guns 'n' Roses.'

'They don't play their kind of music.'

'No, they're much classier.'

'They're goin' to be big. And Jake will be top-dog.'

'What about a dance, Elaine?'

'Of course. Isn't that what everything's about?'

By now, Scorpion Jack were really putting it together – explosively alive and vibrant. It was going to be a great night. A night of celebration. Part of the interim before their dreams would become real, or die.

When the gig was over they went back to Greystones in real style; in the back of the fruit and vegetable van. The band equipment bumped about and Jake told tales of how fame was only around the corner, and that Scorpion Jack weren't too far away from the big time.

None of them disbelieved him. They only hoped it would all come true and that indeed fame was only a few gigs away.

So ended their summer, in hope and belief that everything they wished for would come true.

And they had every right to wish and hope, just as all young people have their hopes and dreams. After all wishing and hoping was part of a young person's spirit; it was their anthem of life.

Luke still went out along the Cliff Walk and its dented cliffs and the gulls perched on the narrow ledges. The area brought back memories of Gavin, Hammer and Jake – even Elaine. The place hadn't changed either. It was wild, lonely, teeming with wildlife. If he were to come back when an old man it would still look the same; the sea, the cliffs, the mountains overhead, the gulls, cormorants, guillemots, linnets, robins, hawks; the ferns; the sun, rain, cloud, clear sky; the paltry few wild goats, the hares; the